THE DISTANCE FROM
FOUR POINTS

Manufactured in the United States of America
ISBN: 978-1-60801-179-7
Copyright © 2020
University of New Orleans Press
2000 Lakeshore Drive
New Orleans, Louisiana 70119

Cover Illustration: "*Taraxacum officinale*" by Walther Otto
Müller (1833–1887), originally appearing in *Köhlers Medizin-al-Pflanzen in naturgetreuen Abbildungen und kurz erläuterndem Texte*
(Germany, 1887) by Hermann Adolph Köhler (1834–1879).

Book and cover design: Alex Dimeff

Printed on acid-free paper
First edition

UNIVERSITY OF NEW ORLEANS PRESS
unopress.org

THE DISTANCE FROM FOUR POINTS

a novel

margo orlando littell

CHAPTER 1

There was a time when, upon pulling into the glittering Steel Star office park, Robin Besher would have wished for more flowers. *Surely,* she would have thought, *we pay enough in retainer fees to warrant more beautiful surroundings.* The landscaping, amid all the brushed chrome and wide parking spaces, was practical at best, with boxwoods under the windows and a few spindly sand cherries. These were the kind of plants that could survive the long Pennsylvania winters, and that was reason enough, she supposed, to have them.

Robin wound her ivory pashmina around her throat and ducked out of the car, keeping her face lowered against January's bitter wind. She wasn't wearing gloves. She'd lost the left hand of her favorite pair, black lambskin with a cashmere lining, and hadn't replaced it. Her nails looked terrible, rough and torn after she'd peeled the gels from her last manicure off herself. This was what she had left. She'd buried her privileged life along with Ray: the Lululemon and Pittsburgh Women's League, the monthly shipments of pricey health shake mix, her home in suburban Mount Rynda with its updated kitchen and Ethan Allen bedroom set—as out of reach now as the callused palms of Ray's hands.

She passed the office where Ray used to visit their accountant. She'd been invited to their meetings, but only as a courtesy, and she'd always had something better to do: clothes to buy for Haley, a dinner to plan, a hair appointment to keep. Now, she wished she'd gone with Ray to every meeting, if only to knock him out the moment he uttered the words *investment property.*

How had Scott Chatham, their attorney, put it to her? The rentals Ray sunk the entirety of their savings into had represented long-term plans. Buying four decrepit properties—two multi-family homes, two single—in a destitute former coal town was a money-making venture that Ray, a high-end contractor, had been well situated to take advantage of. He took a risk. A risk—he'd cashed out their life insurance, believing that, in time, he'd make it all back and more. No one could have predicted that his kayak would overturn on a day no sane person would have been out on the Yough.

Scott, her friends, even her hairdresser expected Robin to be furious, but Robin couldn't explain that it wasn't just that Ray had spent the money. Despite what everyone said about marriage and partnership, it was *his* money, and there had never been much debate between them about that. No, the thing she could never forgive was the town. Ray had bought the properties in Four Points, her hometown, the very place he'd plucked her out of. Now that he was dead, her name was on the deeds. She owned a piece of that place, a burden she had to carry again, twenty years after her escape.

When Robin pulled open the heavy glass door that led to Scott's firm, she met a gust of hot, cedar-scented air. She breathed deeply. The glowing aroma diffuser, the plush carpet, the receptionist with trendy highlights, the jades on her desk—Robin already missed them. This might be her last visit to such an expensive, luxurious office. Scott was being kind, keeping this appointment, fully aware that Robin no longer had any way of paying him. It was a familiar feeling, that dependence.

"Robin." Scott stepped out of his office, extended a hand to welcome her in. "Good to see you. It's a cold one today."

She sat on the leather chair in front of his desk, smoothed her wool slacks. She couldn't quite meet Scott's eye, her attention drifting over his shoulder to familiar surroundings. Rows of dark bookshelves, family photos in gold-plated frames, thick hunter-green draperies over standard-issue corporate windows. She'd seen them countless times before, but they'd never seemed so aggressively showy.

"The orchid bloomed again," she observed, gesturing to a hot-pink flower in a porcelain pot. She'd given it to Scott as a thank you last year for trying to pull strings with her mortgage lender. She should have saved the fifty dollars.

Scott considered the orchid politely, then cleared his throat. "So. Robin." He peered at her, gauging whether she'd make a scene as she had many times before. Of course, Robin no longer sobbed through the meetings. Whatever humiliations she'd endured in this office— the piecing away of the life that had buffered her from all her former desperation—they had all led up to this, the final indignity.

"Call the bank again," she said. "Ask for more time."

Scott's face twitched with pity. "They gave more time. They lowered your rate. You still can't pay the mortgage."

"I can try."

Scott sat back. "Robin. We both know there's no job you can get that'll keep you in that house."

Oh, but she had tried. She'd lasted two weeks behind the register at Giant Eagle. The manager felt bad when he fired her, but Robin couldn't stop herself from crying through every shift. Then she'd gotten a waitressing job at an Olive Garden, but she was decades older than the other servers and couldn't keep up with the dinner rush like she could when she was young and starving. She didn't bother to wait to be fired. She wanted to be the kind of woman who'd hustle when shit hit the fan, but she wasn't. Not when the odds were so clearly stacked against her.

"The house is lost already," Scott said. A single file folder sat on the desk between them. He passed it from one hand to the other, then planted his palm on top.

"There are no saleable assets," he said. "We need to figure out where you're going to go."

"I'll find an apartment. Okay? Something close by so Haley can stay at Our Lady. She's thirteen. I won't make her change schools halfway through the year. I have to get going, Scott. School lets out soon."

She gripped her handbag and stood.

"Sit down."

Scott's desk phone trilled. He glanced at it, discreetly pressed a button to silence the ringing. He flipped open the folder and nudged it toward her. Inside were spread-sheets, pages of them. They'd gone over spreadsheets countless times but always on the computer that sat off to the side—him counseling and her adjusting. Now, in hard copy, they were reality. Nothing left to change.

Scott tilted the first page so that they could both see it. "Look. Rentals in Mount Rynda—the kind you'd be looking for—start at $2,500 a month. That's completely out of reach."

He'd laid it all out in a grid. He'd supposed that she would work as a receptionist—optimistic—and waitress at night, making her $28,000 a year after taxes. There would be less money for Haley's Catholic school tuition. There would be less groceries, less gas, less utilities, less health insurance. All that *less* came down in a stream of red.

When Scott spoke, his voice was even. He delivered hard truths every day. "I'm going to be blunt. You can't afford to stay in Mount Rynda. Do you understand what I'm saying?"

"I don't understand any of this."

"You have to leave."

"Absolutely not."

"The Four Points properties are all you have left, Robin."

"You told me I can't sell them, the condition they're in."

"You can't sell them. But you can live in one of them for free, and they're a way to make a living. Stay with me, Robin." He flipped to the next sheet. "Right now you've got tenants in five units, which comes to $1,900 a month if every tenant pays. You'll live in one empty property and fix up the worst-off apartment."

On the sheet, Robin could see that he expected her to have a tenant by March. Just over a month to fix up a place in God only knew what condition. Well, Robin could imagine. She'd lived in places like that, and she knew nothing about how to make them fit for occupancy. A fixed-up place would get her $450 a month, and Scott had her raising all the rents after half a year. No more than $3,000 a month in rent payments would come in even then, not including upkeep. Her eyes returned to the cells detailing the first empty unit, the place where she was supposed to live.

"You're saying the only place I can go is Four Points?"

"You need to get the rents from Ray's properties. In the meantime, it's a roof over your head. And Haley's."

The mention of Haley was supposed to make her feel guilty, and it did. But there was more at stake, and living in Four Points could only do Haley harm.

"How much do I have to make to come back home?"

"It's not that clear."

"How much?"

Scott sighed. "Ten grand," he said. "You need to sock away ten grand before you can come back here."

"I'll need $10,000?"

"Well, $5,00 for security and first month on a rental. Another $5,000 for you and Haley to live on while you find a job. In the meantime, you can be happy. Make a new life."

"Not in Four Points."

Scott raised his eyebrows. Robin didn't know if it was possible for Scott or anyone else to look into her past life, but she'd never been willing to take the risk. Even directly acknowledging her feelings about Four Points felt dangerous.

"A lot of worse-off places in southwestern P-A," Scott said.

"I grew up there. I made a lot of mistakes."

"We all did. Hell, we were young."

Whatever mistakes Scott had made in his life were nothing close to the things she'd done. She almost wanted to tell him the truth, show him exactly why he had to find another place—another way—for her to live.

Scott straightened the papers in front of him. "Well, I don't know what else to tell you. Haley needs to be your first priority."

"That's exactly why I can't go back."

Scott was trying to help, trying to be a friend to her the way he'd been to Ray, but he didn't know her. No one in Mount Rynda did. He couldn't possibly understand that a choice between Four Points and starving wasn't so easy to make. If she didn't have Haley, there'd be no question: she'd starve.

Scott flipped the last spreadsheet over. On the back, he'd written a name, Tom Frost, and a telephone number.

"Friend of Ray's. Another landlord. He'll be happy to get you set up."

Robin had the distinct feeling that she was being passed to someone else. She supposed that Scott felt he had taken over for Ray, in some unspoken chain of custody. Her whole adult life had been this way. Before Ray, there had been—well, but that was before.

"I'm going to make it right," she said. "I know you don't believe me. I'll go if I have to—but I'll be back in Mount Rynda by spring."

CHAPTER 2

Robin grasped the handle on the storage unit door. She'd sold almost everything she owned, but inside were the few things she couldn't bear to part with. She could see shadows of an oak bed frame, made by Ray, and an heirloom wardrobe from a family member of his she'd never met. In a corner were boxes of her mother-in-law's teacup collection, left to Robin in her will. The teacups were all but worthless, but Ray had insisted the gift was meaningful. Robin didn't have the heart to lug the cups and saucers to Goodwill, but she doubted she'd ever open the boxes again. When she pulled the door down, the steel shutters groaned, the only sound in all the gravel-paved aisles of U-Store-It apart from Haley's hoarse sobs.

For now, they took what they could carry: Their favorite clothes and shoes. The strongbox of important papers and photos. Laptops, phone chargers, stuffed animals, and tchotchkes that Haley, a sentimentalist, couldn't bear to leave behind. Sheets and towels. Some dishware. Two big bags of uneaten, nonperishable food. And, in Robin's purse, an envelope with $3,425 in cash from selling her designer dresses, furniture, and home décor to people in a local swap group.

tea. Friends for twenty years, Robin trusted her. Not enough to tell her everything, but she trusted her.

"Late start?" Steph said.

Robin bit the inside of her lip. She wouldn't, couldn't, lose it now.

"I wanted to drive by and pretend I was coming in for some chardonnay like any other Thursday."

Robin shook her head. She couldn't speak.

"Here," Steph said. "Didn't have time to run it over earlier." She held the bag out to Haley. "Your favorite. Lasagna and caesar salad for tomorrow."

"You didn't have to do that," Robin managed to say.

"Haley," Steph said. "That bag looks heavy for you."

Haley looked down at her hand. "Oh. Yeah." She took the hint and climbed into the passenger seat. Robin watched her secure the bag on her lap, arms wrapped around it protectively.

"Robin." Tears had pooled under Steph's eyes. "I'm worried. Didn't you say you'd rather die than go back to Four Points? Tell me what's happening."

Robin hugged her. The smell of Shalimar was faint in Steph's hair.

"I can't," Robin whispered.

"I'll text you," Steph insisted.

Robin nodded. Without looking back, she got into her car and drove away.

By the time they made it out of Mount Rynda's serpentine streets, it was too dark to see the mountains. Pittsburgh rose around her as she sped down I-376, office towers glowing, the skyline crosscut by the Fort Pitt Bridge. She glimpsed at the Incline inching down the side of Mount Washington. Ray had proposed there. From the top, the city's three rivers were visible— Allegheny, Monongahela, Ohio, all quickly obscured in the rearview mirror by the crowd of stuff that remained of their married life.

When they met, she'd told Ray a story about Four Points that was just wayward enough to be believable. She'd waitressed; she'd skipped a lot of school; she hadn't kept any friends. She'd only tried to tell the full story once, early, when she thought he wanted something like that, something open and complete. *When I was young*, she'd begun, her voice betraying the weight of what would come. He'd held up a hand, briefly covered her mouth with his. *I know you didn't have an easy life*, he'd said. *You don't have to talk about it*. He was afraid of what ghosts she might summon, and he'd chosen not to hear. He hadn't understood what a luxury that was—the decadence of not having to know. She'd taken his words for what they were, both refusal and permission, and held on to her secrets. Ray had needed a certain kind of woman in his life, and Robin was only too happy to slip on a brand new skin. Expensively moisturized, expertly waxed, smooth under silk and cashmere. She'd learned the new rules well. She'd made a good life for Haley, for herself. She wouldn't let Four Points take that away.

Haley was asleep, or pretending to sleep, so Robin turned on the radio and twisted the dial from NPR to country. She used to know every song, every word, every moony story of heartbreak and pain. Now, the words were as unfamiliar as dreams.

Ahead, boring through the mountain, was the Fort Pitt Tunnel, narrow and amber-lit, two lanes split by double lines. Robin didn't slow as she tipped the car in. After a few yards, the radio faded to a silence as heavy as water in her ears.

The whooshing of air surrounded the car like an ocean. The tunnel was still familiar, though Robin had done everything in her power to avoid driving this way again. She'd made this drive once already, going the opposite way, with Ray in the driver's seat. She'd gone through hell to get there—to the passenger seat of Ray's car. Now all she'd earned had been ripped away, and the steering wheel hummed in her hands.

Returning to Four Points was a new low, but she hadn't reached the bottom yet. Robin tried not to imagine the numerous ways her life—what was left of it—could fall even further apart. What would she do if she and Haley were out shopping, and she saw one of the men who used to visit her in the basement of Cindy Sweeney's house on Whistlestop Road? She'd changed a lot in twenty years but maybe not enough. She didn't want to explain to Haley that the world is cruel for some girls, that even if they work themselves to the bone, in the end it's sometimes just easier to sell sex. Sometimes the only choice available is between bad and worse. She'd been a poor, desperate teenager, but she couldn't ask Haley to understand and accept the reality she herself couldn't stomach. The world wasn't fair. Life wasn't fair. These were the lessons she didn't want to teach.

Worse was the knowledge that, once she was in familiar Four Points places—passing the diaper aisle of the Shop 'n Save or the free clinic with all the sniffling, coughing infants—grief might overwhelm her. Trevor, her son, had been nine months old when he died. Robin had been nineteen. Only with his death—the official cause was SIDS—did Four Points really change for her. She had to leave, not letting the tragedy go but burying it along with the rest of her past. Even at forty-three, she felt the absence of Trevor from the world like a missing peak from the Laurel Mountains, changing everything: wind, shadows, light. Another thing Haley could never know. A child shouldn't witness that kind of sadness in her mother.

The radio lost its static. They were out of the tunnel, on the Turnpike, heading south. Ray's tool box rattled behind her as she drove, the tools heavy as old bones.

*   *   *

It was 1:00 a.m. when they finally slid into Four Points. No other cars stalked the streets at this hour, and the dark quiet was deepened by the shallow breaths of Haley sleeping beside her. Robin was alert at the wheel, every nerve thrumming.

After the exit, a ten-minute drive along desolate, hilly roads—a trailer here and there in the fields, a few spot-lit American flags—took them into town. The familiar weathered sign: *Welcome to Four Points, Population: 5,000.* Robin crossed Ember Street, a sorry stretch of empty storefronts, and drove two minutes to the leaning, beige-sided ranch on Dandelion Drive that she and Haley would call home. She *owned* this house: a cruel joke. It was in the middle of a street of small ranches. In the moonlight, they all had the same dull glow. Robin's was clearly the block's disgrace, aggressively neglected, wearing its care-less vacancy like a gruesomely scarred, unpatched eye.

Beside her, Haley stirred, lifted her head from the ski jacket balled against her door. She reflexively fin-ger-combed her flyaway hair into a ponytail, her glittery lavender nail polish winking in the dashboard lights.

"Where are we?"

"Dandelion Drive." Robin refused to say *home*.

She found the plastic-tagged key in her purse. Ray's handwriting: *25 Dandelion*. She stepped out of the car and onto the cement slab out front and held the flimsy aluminum screen door open against her hip. When she jiggled the key in the lock and pushed, the knob came off in her hand.

"Jesus," Haley said.

"Language," Robin said, but it was a reflex. There was no appropriate reaction, not tonight.

Robin felt for a light switch and flicked on a dim, bare bulb overhead. They were standing in a small room with a suggestion of furniture—a stained, sagging couch, a white plastic coffee table, and a paisley bedsheet nailed over the single window, which was broken. The floor was sheathed in filthy linoleum, peeling at the edges. There was no heat.

Haley walked to the middle of the room. She looked up. On the ceiling was a large brown water stain.

"I thought you said it was furnished," she said.

"That's what Scott told me. I guess it is, sort of."

The house was small. Beyond the living room where they stood was the kitchen, and to the left was a short hallway with two bedrooms and a bathroom between. The white paint on the walls was dingy, and dirt and grease were so thick on the floor that they had depth and texture. On the wall was a thermostat. Robin twisted it to seventy, praying. She led Haley into the kitchen, where a card table with four metal folding chairs was jammed between the refrigerator and the wall. In the sink was a dead cockroach, its legs bent into its body. When Robin turned the water on, it flipped to its feet and skittered into the drain. They both screamed.

"Let's unload the car," Robin said when her heart stopped pounding.

Piece by piece, they emptied the trunk, piling their belongings beside the couch. Robin put the bags of food in the kitchen, not daring to open the cupboards tonight—she couldn't face any fresh horrors. She tore open the box holding the sheets and blankets and took them in her arms. Both bedrooms were cheaply wood-paneled and linoleum-floored, each single window sheathed in a great pouf of torn white polyester— long, ruffly curtains meant for much larger windows. Only one of the two bedrooms had a bed: a bare, stained, full-size mattress on a metal frame. Robin covered it with every sheet, blanket, and towel she'd brought.

Next: the broken window.

"I'll be right back," she told Haley.

She went to the car, opened the back door. The ceiling light shone directly on Ray's tool box. For a moment, she was overcome with anguish. She bent over, put both hands on the leather seat. She was failing. Had failed. She'd lost their home, yanked Haley away from everything she knew and loved, and what she'd offered in its place was—this. She was a terrible mother. Selfish. She should have driven to Four Points last week alone and prepared the house for their arrival. She could have brought a little furniture, arranged to fix the window, bleached and dusted every surface. Or—seeing what it was like—she could have figured out another place for them to stay. Instead, she'd dug in her heels, putting off her return until the last possible moment. Now here she was, without another option. Robin peered into the car as though Ray himself would manifest and save them both.

Robin unlatched Ray's tool box. A hammer, three wrenches, a complicated screwdriver with a set of thirty heads. A cordless drill and charger. Nails, screws, bolts of all kinds. Then she saw them, almost hidden by the drill: two thick rolls of heavy-duty duct tape.

Nearby, a dog growled, and some cold creature rustled in the hedges. She straightened, slid the rolls onto her wrist. Held them aloft, triumphant, to show Haley as she walked inside.

"Dad's tool box," Robin said.

There would never be an end to the things that made them cry.

Haley watched as Robin duct-taped a flattened moving box over the window. She guided tape along the edges of the cardboard and tore the strips with her teeth. The makeshift cover would have to do. Hot air gusted from a floor vent. The furnace worked.

Though it was too late for deep cleaning, Robin stalked each room with a rag and a bottle of Lysol all-purpose spray and wiped down anything she and Haley might touch. Door frames, door knobs, light switches—erasing previous tenants' fingerprints along with her own.

The air now smelled of mildew and lemon disinfectant. And grease, dust, old laundry. As she crawled into bed, Robin brushed crumbs and strangers' hair from the bottoms of her socks. People lived like this, with so little care for their surroundings. She'd forgotten. Every woman she knew in Mount Rynda had a biweekly housecleaner.

Haley wavered at the edge of the bedroom door. "This place is disgusting," she said.

Robin turned onto her back, hoping the mattress springs wouldn't prod so painfully. "Yes," she said.

Haley climbed into bed. She reached over and took Robin's hand, holding on for dear life.

*   *   *

Robin lay still, listening. The furnace ticked on somewhere below them. Heat gusted, briefly, from floor vents. Through the thin walls and single-pane windows, nothing. The neighborhood slept.

Robin took deep, deliberate breaths—inhale five, exhale eight—but her heart kept pounding hard enough to hurt her ribs. The first memory to rush in was the feel of Cindy's hair: coarse with an almost sticky chemical sheen. Like Barbie hair. Every couple of weeks, Robin helped Cindy rinse new purple-auburn Clairol gel from her hair into the basement bathroom sink. The stained water swirled down the drain like blood. Robin used to dye her hair too—her color was more dramatic, an indigo-shadowed black that swallowed the light, made her capable of things, untouchable even when being touched.

The memory of hair dye—the eggy, sweet smell—was physical. Robin was back in that bathroom, pink-painted cement walls and faded silk flowers on the sill of the tiny glass-block window.

Robin was living with Cindy back then, in a house on Whistlestop Road, renting a room from Cindy's mother, Rochelle. She'd left home when her drunk mother attacked her in her sleep, pummeling her with a two-liter of Pepsi—the final outrage after life with an addict's vitriol. Robin waitressed every single night at the Rowdy Buck, but unless she dropped out of school, she wouldn't be able to earn enough money to rent a room and keep herself fed. She didn't want to drop out. Too much like her mother. But she skipped school now and then to pick up a double shift.

Rochelle had scoffed at Robin's frantic nighttime waitressing when she first moved in.

"Working yourself to death, for what?" she'd asked. "Easier ways to make money than that. Cin knows. Hell, I do too."

That was the last Rochelle ever said of it. Cindy showed her the twenties wrapped with a hair band in her purse. When Rochelle saw that Robin had cut back her shifts, she raised her rent with a smile and expected it in full on the first of the month.

The sound of footsteps on the stairs. The boys waiting when the girls emerged from the bathroom, their hair damp, Robin's hands stained sunset orange, Cindy's blue-black. Rochelle never asked the boys questions, who they were or what they wanted. She just let them in and sent them to the cellar. It didn't really matter who got who. Mostly, though, the boys wanted Cindy.

Sometimes the guys who came for Cindy didn't expect to find Robin. The surprise, the sense of wary discovery, kept them coming back. She didn't think too much about who they were as long as they paid for her time. She mostly knew the guys she serviced, men who might be pathetic but weren't, as a rule, dangerous. The older ones—from the bars, the mines, the ones best met in a crowded place instead of an isolated basement— were usually there for Cindy. Everyone at school knew, but they mostly left Robin alone. Cindy was the girl who had *whore* scrawled on her locker, who fought in the hallways, who met her enemies behind the Dairy Queen with a circle of kids ready to watch and cheer. She was tough: big-boned and muscular, unafraid to wrap a ponytail around her wrist and go for the nose. She always smelled of cigarettes and hairspray. She wasn't pretty, but boys liked being afraid of her.

When Robin started, she'd willingly followed Cindy's lead, expecting an innate inner hustle to reveal itself and get her through. It never had. She'd found her own way to survive. Passing through the doorway and descending the stairway to the basement, she'd convinced herself it was a kind of magical threshold, transforming her into someone else during the fumbling encroachments on her body.

Now, she found herself unable to tap into that long-ago technique. She could no longer abandon herself—she had Haley. She'd passed through no magical threshold as she crossed from Mount Rynda to Four Points. She was the same on the other side. Beside her, Haley breathed.

CHAPTER 3

The morning light through the crooked plastic venetian blinds looked exactly as it used to: sallow and thin, filtered through something grittier than the gray dust coating the glass. Haley was still sleeping, her long hair spilling over the edge of her pillow, into the stretched-out neck of her old unicorn sweatshirt.

Robin leaned over. On her phone, a string of texts appeared from Steph. *How are you? How's the place? How's Haley?* Hearts, a kiss-blowing emoji face, a tear. *Call me. Let me know how you're doing. I found one of your hair wraps this morning at the gym.* Robin deleted the thread without replying.

She slipped out of bed. In the bathroom, she swallowed a preemptive Advil with a gulp of water from the sink, girding herself for her first rent collection day. Since Robin had never met her tenants and—more urgently—had never even visited the properties, today she'd collect her money door to door. In the future, the tenants would come to her.

She brushed her teeth, washed her face, and reluctantly looked in the mirror. She smoothed her hair. Skimming the chestnut were a few gray strands, thin as fibers, which came free with barely a tug. Endless others winked when she changed the part in her hair. Pointless to keep plucking. The grays outpaced any hope of affording a cut-and-color. Her hair had always been very long, but it was more witchy than sultry now without weekly deep conditioning. Maybe she'd chop it. She dabbed concealer under her unlined eyes, no match for the shadows. She uncapped her favorite Clinique lipstick, Plum Brandy. The color was wrong here, too bright. She dropped it into her makeup bag and left her lips plain. Anyway, her tenants would only see her as another landlord with her palm open, angling for a glimpse of the thermostat or evidence of unauthorized pets.

At breakfast, she passed Haley a box of Cheerios from across the kitchen table. In the light of day, the house was less nightmarish. The counters were clean, the water and electricity worked. Robin could be grateful for small things. Well, if not exactly grateful, perhaps a little relieved. That cockroach in the sink had to have been a stray, taking advantage of a long-empty home, not an emissary from a larger colony. Maybe next weekend she and Haley could drive back to U-Store-It, retrieve a bureau and an end table, the good coffeemaker and the toaster. Some of their familiar things might help make Dandelion Drive less terrible.

Haley waggled her phone. "Are we getting Wi-Fi?"

Robin shook her head. She wouldn't tell Haley yet that she'd soon have to give up her phone plan—at least, the parts that were interesting to a thirteen-year-old. Haley slid the phone into her backpack.

"Are you still doing the rent thing today?" Haley asked.

"I wish I wasn't."

"Can't they keep sending it to Scott?"

"I need to see these properties. I'll be back by the time you get home from school."

At the door, Haley slumped against Robin, pressing her forehead into Robin's shoulder. "I don't want to go. You should homeschool me."

Robin smoothed Haley's hair. It was fine and silky, still like a child's.

"Just do your work," Robin said. "You won't even be there next year, so get through the next couple of months as best you can."

"Morgan said I could stay with her during the week. Why can't I?"

"We're a team," Robin said. "We stay together." They'd had this conversation only about a hundred times. "Now go before you miss the bus. I can't wait to hear about it."

Robin couldn't explain why Heather Lutz's invitation had riled her so much. Inviting Haley—her daughter's best friend—to spend Monday through Friday with them in Mount Rynda to finish out the school year was shockingly generous. Refusing had been awkward, but leaving Haley behind was impossible. Even if she could bear the separation, she couldn't afford to keep Haley at Our Lady. Heather Lutz and the other Mount Rynda women had no idea what Robin was facing, which wasn't entirely their fault. By giving only vague explanations for her move, Robin had let them believe she was undertaking a lucrative property development project on Ray's behalf.

Robin watched Haley until the bus eased to a stop. Of course Haley had to go to school. Establishing new routines was crucial. Meanwhile, the shape of Robin's own days remained hazy. Today, at least, she knew what she had to do. She quickly collected her file folders and purse and put on her shoes and coat.

February 1, deep winter. Morning was black and bitter. Sleet chilled her to the bone. She blasted the car heater, the air rustling papers in the bulging file beside her. The spreadsheet listed four addresses: Nettle Street, Foxtail Street, East Green Street, Dandelion Drive. She and Haley were staying in the Dandelion property, and there were six other rental units: Foxtail Street, a single-family home; Nettle Street, a duplex; East Green, split—somehow—into three apartments.

Her first stop: Sheetz, for a tank of gas and an eighty-nine-cent cup of over-roasted coffee. When she went inside to pay, the cashier smiled as he extended the receipt, sliding his fingers over hers. Sleepy, bloodshot eyes, uncombed hair, a bit of blond chest hair and leathered skin visible at his throat.

"Anything else?" he said.

"That's it." She turned toward the door.

"Hey," he called. "We know each other?"

Robin gave a half-glance over her shoulder, not meeting his eye. "I'm not from around here," she said. Her mind spun—he was about her age, forty and change. Something about the worn, rough skin of his neck, his suggestive, drooping eyes, was slightly familiar. She could know him. She could. She may have, long ago, in another lifetime lived within this town but surely, also, in another universe entirely—

She locked herself hastily in the car, sloshing coffee onto her hand. Every terrible, unwanted thing was exactly the way it was before. She still felt the cashier's rough, warm fingers. She still smelled his cigarettes. He'd sensed something about her. She forced herself to drive out of the parking lot and onto the road, gripping the wheel to stop her shaking.

She started off easy, 3201 Foxtail, a two-bedroom, aluminum-sided bungalow with a green-tinged roof. Moss? Mold? Roofs weren't supposed to be green. Large swaths of siding were dingy gray. The small front yard was split by a walkway leading to neatly trimmed evergreen bushes and a porch with a white wicker chair. She glanced at the spreadsheet: Deirdre Boone, tenant for five years, $500 per month in rent—the highest of all Robin's tenants. The house was habitable and apparently cared for.

Deirdre opened the door before Robin could knock. No makeup, graying light-brown hair cut bluntly around her face. She walked with the slight stoop of a woman who spent too much of each day on her feet. Though her smile was friendly enough, her gaze was appraising and doubtful.

According to the spreadsheet, she'd never been late on rent, never caused any problems. Deirdre's hand was plain and square with ragged fingernails, not so much rough as simply firm in Robin's own.

"It's real nice to meet you," she said. "Wanted to say I'm sorry. Ray was a good person, not like some of the other landlords around here. I called with a problem, he took care of it. Never had to call twice." She tilted her head slightly, her eyes flicking over Robin's Sorels, her slim black North Face. "Hope that won't change."

Robin shook her head vigorously. "Of course not. I'm right here if you need me." She gave what she hoped was a competent smile.

"Alright. Thanks," Deirdre said. "Come in for a sec."

Robin followed Deirdre toward the kitchen.

"Get ready for this," Deirdre said. "Here we go—*buongiorno!*"

A previous tenant had embellished the long wall of the kitchen with a large painted scene of mountains rising behind a blue lake. Dotting the water were boats with crisp white sails and yachts with crudely rendered portholes. In the far-left foreground were the crowded, uneven rooftops of an old stone village, shutters flung open to the air.

"They told me it's supposed to be Lake Como. That's in Italy." Deirdre stopped at the threshold, framed the wall with her hands. "Don't turn your head," she said. "Don't move your eyes."

Margo Orlando Littell

Robin did as she was told. She made a frame with her raised hands. Dimming the chipped blue of the lake was the scum of dirt and cooking oil. On the ceiling closest to the solitary stove, paint was peeling, loosened by steam from a thousand boiling pots. Streaks of nicotine-stained water spidered into the treetops lining the Alps.

"I love it," Deirdre was saying. "It's what made me take the house, even though it didn't even have a working sink at the time. 'I'll have one by the weekend,' Ray kept saying, but who believes a landlord? I saw the wall and said okay."

"And you got a sink."

"I did. Ray kept his word."

Deirdre handed over a sealed white envelope, thick with cash. "Here you go," she said. "One more thing. I hate to bother you right away, but Ray did promise to take care of the mildew in the bathroom. He nailed up a shower curtain to keep the wall dry and said he'd tile. It was supposed to happen last year, but."

"I'll do it," Robin said. "If Ray promised, it must be important."

"Thanks so much."

Back in the car, Robin's mind raced. She couldn't even begin to imagine how to tile a shower. She'd figure it out. She'd have to. She'd do whatever she had to do to get out of there.

The yellow brick duplex on Nettle Street wasn't as nice as the Foxtail property, though lights in the windows of both sides made it almost friendly. Shingles were missing from the roof. Fat prickly shrubs had grown wild, their sharp bare branches pushing against the cinderblocks that led to the porch. A nun named Sister Eileen lived in the left-hand side, 1118 Nettle, paying $400 per month in rent.

Robin knocked. After a long minute, a crop-haired nun in a plain skirt and blouse opened the door.

"Ah, yes, rent day," she said in greeting. She reached over, patted Robin's arm. "I'm so sorry to hear about your husband. He was a good landlord. Always sent someone over when I had problems. Stepping in must be hard for you."

"Yes," Robin said. She touched each eye with a bent knuckle, resisting an urge to break down. "We're still reeling, I think. The death, losing the house, coming back to Four Points." She was saying too much. The nun's steady, calm-gazing presence somehow invited confession.

"Please let me help in any way I can," said Sister Eileen.

"I appreciate that."

There was a pause. A teenage girl teetered out of a house across the street, thigh-high black boots covering bare legs, and got into a car idling at the curb, her eyes never leaving her phone. Sister Eileen frowned.

"I'm so sorry," she said. "I don't have my rent. The diocese provides my living expenses, and there's a backlog." She sighed. "I'm not supposed to be in a rental property. I should be in the religious housing next to the school, but those rooms are taken right now by Romanian missionaries. It's a complicated situation. They weren't supposed to stay on this long." She waved a hand. "So here I am, in your duplex. Ray said we could go month to month, and I'm going on fourteen months now."

"It's fine," Robin said. "Please don't worry. Pay whenever you can." She needed that rent money, really needed it, but part of her felt she owed something to Sister Eileen—some debt, some penance. She pushed the idea away as she crossed the porch to the door of 1118 ½. Another $400 on the line. Robin steeled herself and knocked.

"Hello, hello!" A bright-eyed woman opened the door and grabbed Robin's hand.

"I'm Anne Sackett," she announced. "And you're the new landlord!" She was wearing a kimono-style robe in a vibrant red floral print, slippers with rubber soles. Her entire forehead was covered by an auburn permanent-wave wig. "Now don't move," she said. She ducked inside and emerged with a plastic bag and a lipsticky, eye-wrinkling smile. "This is just to say—welcome." She pressed the bag toward Robin. "I always gave Ray a little something extra, and I wanted to do the same for you."

She watched Robin expectantly. Her glasses enlarged her eyes, making them seem insect-like. Robin reached into the bag and pulled out a plastic tube of combs, multi-colored and multi-sized, the top of the tube secured with clear tape. Anne smiled again, her forehead sliding into her wig.

"There's a gold one in there, you see it? I thought you might like the gold one."

"Thank you. So much," Robin said.

Anne nodded importantly. "You seem like a lovely person, Robin," she said. "I, for one, am so glad you're here."

The tube of combs left a tacky residue on Robin's fingers when she tucked it into her purse, but she appreciated the gesture of goodwill. She felt a sudden, sweeping confidence that Ray knew what he was doing. He wouldn't have been foolish enough to rent to destructive young hoodlums or wild-eyed addicts. Anne was sweet, harmless. Eager to please.

"I'll collect your rent while I'm here," Robin said.

"Ah, right, the first. The thing is, I don't have it ready," Anne said. "I'll get it to you soon, if that's okay. I just don't have it right now."

"When will you have it?"

"Soon. Really soon. Today snuck up on me. I'm sorry. You can trust me, you've known me for years, haven't you? Well, Ray has."

"Bring it as soon as you can, Anne."

"Of course, Robin. Tell you what. Come by tomorrow. Late afternoon, four-ish. Alright? Alright?"

Robin fell into the driver's seat of her Highlander. Between Anne and Sister Eileen, she was $800 down. She almost couldn't believe this was happening. There was never a problem in the months when Scott Chatham was collecting the rents by mail. Clearly, she lacked authority.

When Robin arrived at the final property, she was immediately grateful she hadn't visited East Green Street first. The East Green triplex was a dismal wreck, with warped gray siding and two boarded windows. A wheel-less car sat on cinderblocks in the driveway. The porch was a tangle of plastic folding chairs, a couple of tray tables, and a rusty bug zapper. In a crooked line by the door were three mailboxes. This was the kind of property people pointed to when they complained about slumlords. Defeat sank heavy in Robin's chest.

Two of the apartments were rented for $300 each by brothers named Damien and Kevin Trundel. The third unit was empty—had been for a while, according to the spreadsheet. Robin fished for the master key on a heavy ring, full almost to capacity.

Inside, wan gray light trickled in through the front door windowpane, enough to show that the hallway desperately needed new paint. The maroon carpet on the stairs, sloppily installed with visible staples, was worn nearly through. The carpet filled the hallway to the two doors on either side. Metal numbers—1, 2—hung on each of the doors. She knocked on both at once.

The Trundel brothers could have been twins, with shaggy dark hair under camouflage ball caps with logos Robin didn't recognize. They both wore heavy work boots and untucked plaid flannel shirts. They offered only mumbled hellos, legs spread wide, blocking as much of their doorways as possible. However, they paid their rent in full—all cash, no envelope, just wads of bills from their jeans pockets—and seemed sane enough.

The empty unit was upstairs. Robin avoided the railing, feeling the funhouse slope of the staircase in the awkward angling of her feet. At the top, she reached for her key, but the apartment door swung inward, unlocked.

The apartment had been trashed. Gashes were torn in the walls. Garbage was strewn across the floor. Dark stains and thick clumps of black hair shadowed the threadbare carpet. The doorframe between the living room and bedroom had been ripped off. Many of the dropped-ceiling tiles, stained gold and brown, teetered precariously from bent metal framing. An acrid smell—urine, rotten food—was inescapable.

According to the spreadsheet, the apartment had been empty for over two years, but in the kitchen was eerie evidence of recent life: a few hunting magazines on the counter, beer cans in the sink, an open soup can by the stove. A squatter. Definitely. Robin couldn't imagine why the Trundel brothers hadn't said anything. Warm air began to pour from an uncovered floor vent—*the heat was on in this apartment*—and Robin, light-headed, leaned against a ruined wall.

She was so angry at Ray, had been for months. At the moment, however, she was most angry at this squatter, whoever he was. The squatter had taken advantage—maybe he'd heard about Ray's death and knew he wouldn't get caught anytime soon. Ray deserved more than that. Robin knew how Ray was, how smoothly he made connections. He was used to dealing with a lot of people as a contractor, needing them to do what he wanted by a certain day and at a certain price. Electricians and plumbers and demolition teams. Clients who needed subtle suggestions for larger additions, fancier kitchens. Imagining Ray being exploited hurt her, deep in the place that missed Ray despite everything.

Robin tried to take a few deep breaths. Scott hadn't said anything about this level of ruin. He likely didn't realize that his talk of "fixing things up" and "getting tenants in the properties" didn't apply here.

She switched the thermostat to low, as low as she could stand to keep the pipes from freezing. She jiggled the doorknob, trying to engage the lock, but it was useless. Well, there was no more damage to fear. She had to get going. Haley was waiting for her at Dandelion Drive. Outside the property, Damien and Kevin Trundel were opening the doors of their truck.

"Wait," Robin called. The brothers watched as Robin approached.

"Sorry to bother you again," she said. "I was just in number three. Did you know someone was living there?"

The brothers glanced at each other.

"Yeah, we knew," Damien said.

"Why didn't you tell Ray?"

"It was after Ray—passed. Kevin called the guy we sent the rent to, and he said keep an eye on it."

"You called Scott Chatham? He knew someone was squatting here?"

Kevin shrugged. "He didn't care too much long as the place didn't burn down. The guy didn't bother us none, so we let it be. When he got that dog and the smell got bad, we took care of it."

"What do you mean, you took care of it?"

"You know, went up there."

"And did what?"

"Just—went up there. Said he should move on."

"And that's it?"

"Let him know we was serious."

Robin could imagine too well the brothers, tall in their heavy boots, the gun rack on their truck. What would have been a lengthy process of legal action and eviction had been taken care of by the Trundels in five minutes. So Scott Chatham understood something about Four Points after all.

"Whoever it was trashed the place," Robin said.

Damien shrugged. "Yeah, we figured."

They'd offer nothing else. Hers was the only disbelief. She drove back to Dandelion Drive, feeling farther away from Mount Rynda than ever. The life she'd made there had surely been nothing more than an illusion. When the light changed, it was gone.

*   *   *

Robin took another Advil and poured a glass of wine. The winter gloom hid the fact that it wasn't even yet five o'clock. It could've been worse. She'd been expecting some version of the Laurel Estates trailer park crowd from her childhood. Rough, mean. Aggressive dogs, dirty kids, forties on the windowsills. These people— the Trundels, the nun, Deirdre, even Anne—were manageable. Still, Anne and Sister Eileen hadn't paid their rent. Two tenants, $800.

Robin texted Scott.

Thanks for telling me about the squatter, she tapped, then tossed her phone on the table. Scott didn't respond. She hadn't expected him to.

She took a long drink of wine, the last bottle left from Mount Rynda—she couldn't afford any more, so she'd damn well enjoy it—and opened the shoebox where she'd stuffed the cash from the day. Without thinking, she laid it out on the coffee table, instinctively separating the bills and shuffling them to face the same direction. She tamped the stacks longways, then sideways, deftly evening the edges with an open palm. She rarely dealt with cash in Mount Rynda—maybe a hundred at a time from the ATM—but it came back to her, the cottony softness of the bills, the way even the most wrinkled ones welcomed their neat place in the pile. The memory was unwelcome, the feel of the thick stack in her fist.

When she tallied the cash in her hand and recorded it on the spreadsheet glowing on her laptop, she watched as calculations were performed automatically, turning text from black to red. Robin feared an errant keystroke would erase the whole thing. She tried to make sense of it, the notes and columns, the figures and sums and dates. Best case, when all her tenants paid, she'd bring in $1,900 every month. This month, so far, she had $1,100. With $900 in mortgage payments, that meant she had $200 to put aside. If anything went wrong, a leaky faucet, a clogged drain, a bird cracking a window with its misguided, unfortunate skull—

She didn't bother opening the sheet titled "Get Back Home." Scott had said she'd need $10,000—absurd even if all her tenants paid. Trying to save even half that much would be a daily struggle as she scrimped and pinched her way into a security deposit and first month on the distant outskirts of Mount Rynda.

She was surprised at how easily the high-wire calculations returned. She hadn't been extravagant in Mount Rynda, hadn't wiled away the school-day hours shopping at the nearby Galleria as so many of her women friends did, collecting Longchamp totes in multiple colors and mooning over Schumacher Hothouse Flower drapery fabric at $300 a yard. Undeniably, though, she'd let her thriftiness slide. She carried her own burgundy Longchamp with a specially-designed organizing caddy bisecting its interior. Her yoga pants were made from recycled plastic water bottles and cost $89 a pair. She'd changed her perfume with the seasons. She'd spent the past twenty years not pinching pennies, assuming that their life was built to accommodate indulgences without complex budget adjustments. She never had to skip a phone payment to fill a prescription, substitute a car repair for groceries. Now, just like when she was young, she was keeping her hard-earned money in a shoebox, hoping the shallow well of bills wouldn't run dry. It was a mindset of scarcity. Robin reached for it, stacked it in the box alongside the cash.

What she needed to do was put Haley in public school—an intolerable idea. Minimizing the influence of Four Points on Haley was as important, or more, as saving every penny. Catholic school was a buffer. Robin couldn't let her daughter walk the same halls she had. Haley already had questions about Robin as a teenager and was dissatisfied with Robin's claims that she remembered little about her early years. Keeping Haley separate from the past was the only way to keep her safe.

For the moment, the most urgent matter was collecting Anne's and Sister Eileen's rents. That was the clear, true thing these rows and columns showed. When she tried to calm her fears of financial ruin by opening a clean, fresh doc sheet for a to-do list, she felt even worse. She had no idea what to write. She needed so very badly to make people pay. She needed to make East Green livable. She may as well have been asking herself to spin straw into gold—without any straw or spinning wheel.

A calendar reminder buzzed on her phone: Saturday, 8:00 p.m., a Landlord Association meeting. Yes: the landlords. Tom Frost and others. She swallowed the rest of her wine and did her best to slow her breathing. She'd find the help she needed among her own kind.

CHAPTER 4

A whole day loomed before the Landlord Association meeting Saturday evening. Robin made some instant coffee and woke Haley. Deirdre had said she'd be at work, so this was a good time for Robin to get her first maintenance job done. Tiling Deirdre's shower wasn't a top priority, but Ray had promised. Besides, Robin wasn't sure what, exactly, qualified as *priority* in the landlording world. Helping a tenant might be exactly how she was supposed to spend her first weekend in Four Points.

Robin opened Deirdre's house with her key and led Haley to the bathroom, where the walls were feathery with peeling paint. Nailed to the wall above the tub was a white plastic shower curtain, shadowed with black mildew.

"Ick," Haley said.

"You're telling me."

The problem, Deirdre had said, was rot. Without tiling in the shower, hot water against the painted plaster wall had resulted in more than one section collapsing into the bathtub. The shower curtain Ray had hung to protect the wall had never been a perfect solution, or even a very good one. Though the wall didn't get drenched with water, the curtain trapped heat and moisture, cultivating the spores. The entire stretch of plaster was ready to crumble.

"What do you have to do?" Haley asked.

"Tile the walls. Not all the way, just to right above the shower head."

"Do you know how to do that?"

"Nope."

"Are you going to call someone?"

"We can figure it out, don't you think?"

Haley gave her a withering look. "Give me your phone." She tapped at the screen. "Here."

They leaned close together over a tiny video. *Today we're going to tile a bathroom wall*, said a bearded man in a plaid shirt, going on to talk about measurements, supplies, and preparations. Robin watched to the end, then started back from the beginning and jotted notes on a piece of paper.

"Let's get to Home Depot," she said.

Robin entered the local store furtively, expecting to draw laughter from the men with trolleys piled with boards and paint cans. With four properties, though, she had as much right to be there as anyone. List in hand, her budget zero, Robin steered Haley to the cheapest white tiles, four dollars a square foot. They put six boxes into the cart, adding an extra ten percent as the man on YouTube suggested. One aisle over, Robin found tile adhesive, grout, a trowel, a notched spreader, and a package of sponges. On a whim, as a gesture of goodwill, she picked out a fresh new shower curtain and liner—the curtain plain pleated white, the liner clear as ice. When she paid for her purchases, the cashier didn't smirk or scoff. Robin emerged from the store emboldened.

Back at Deirdre's, while Robin cleared space in the bathroom, Haley explored the house.

"Whoa," she said. "Mom, come here."

She was examining a collection of angels on a cloth-covered table. The angels were different colors and sizes, made mostly from porcelain but also clay, wood, glass, even a dried, painted corn husk. All were cherubs. Haley examined them as Robin lugged the first load of tiles into the bathroom.

"Seventy-six," Haley said, joining Robin with another box of tiles. "Seventy-six dead kids."

She meant it as a joke, but neither of them laughed.

Robin used the end of a hammer to pry the nails from the wall-covering shower curtain, grimacing as it crumbled into the tub. Ray must have known this makeshift barrier was worse than temporary, that tiling was inevitable. Now Robin was taking that step, cracking the lid from a bucket of adhesive. Behind her, Haley was stuffing the curtain into a trash bag, touching it only with paper towels, her face in a grimace.

"This is so, so gross."

It *was* gross, crouched with her trowel in Deirdre's bathtub, soap scum on the sides and hair in the drain.

"Tiles," Robin said. Haley rested a stack at Robin's feet. She laid them as evenly as she could over the adhesive, across the length of the tub. When Haley got bored with handing over tiles, she took the new shower curtain into Deirdre's bedroom and unfolded it on the bed, smoothing the wrinkles with her palm.

"Thanks for coming with me today," Robin said when she wandered back in.

Haley shrugged. "Sure."

"How's school?"

"Ridiculous. But fine."

"Why? What's happening?"

"Mean girl stuff," Haley said. "This girl Amber doesn't like me."

"What'd she do?"

"She called me a bitch because a boy she likes talked to me at lunch."

Robin lowered her trowel. "What? Haley, that's terrible."

"It's no big deal. She's mean to everyone. This other girl, Kelsey, said she lives in a trailer park."

"Haley." Robin was torn. She ought to tell Haley that being from a trailer park didn't make you worse than anyone else, that stereotypes were ugly and damaging. The world was filled with different people, different homes, different kinds of lives, none better or worse than any other. A good mother would say all this, steer her daughter toward kindness. But as she crouched in Deirdre's bathtub in a town she despised, Robin found the teachable moment out of reach. She couldn't make the words come out, not when the trailer parks she grew up in weren't even five miles away.

"Just do your work and stay out of it," Robin said. "You're privileged, Haley, you understand that. You have advantages these other girls don't have."

"Advantages like our beautiful new house?"

"This is temporary," Robin said tightly. "I'm doing the best I can, Haley, with your father gone."

"Dad would freak if he saw the school. No one can sit by the radiator because hot steam shoots out."

Ray had become a contractor superhero to Haley, with the power to provide a good home and a good life. Robin, it seemed, could only provide the house on Dandelion Drive.

"You won't have to worry for long," Robin said. She tried not to think about the spreadsheet.

They worked the rest of the afternoon. By four, the shower was tiled. It wasn't perfect, but the wall was protected. Robin cleaned the trowel and spreader and put them in Ray's tool box. Any satisfaction she may have felt dissolved in the accounting: the project had cost $150. Her body ached. Grout thickened her nails and dotted the hair at her temples, and she'd sliced her palm on a piece of broken tile. Home again, she waited for a phone call of thanks from Deirdre, but none came.

*   *   *

That evening, Robin drove to the Way Car, a bar in the decrepit Riverside Hotel by the Yough owned by Tom Frost. The hotel had been condemned when Robin was a kid, and it hadn't improved much aside from the Coors sign blazing in the window. Robin parked in the busy-looking lot beside the bar, wary of walking alone to the entrance. A wall of hot cigarette smoke hit her eyes when she pulled open the plate-glass door.

From a long table at the back of the room, a man waved her over, then stood and met her halfway. He was tall, probably six-three, with a firm, square jaw. His hair was so perfectly salt-and-peppered Robin knew immediately he used Touch of Gray.

"Robin. I'm Tom Frost." He embraced her, his rough canvas coat smelling of latex paint. "Let me get a look at you." Tom held her at arm's length, his eyes drifting over her body. Robin regretted the gray V-neck cashmere, the slouchy black suede boots. She'd wanted to make an effort.

"A Four Points beauty," Tom announced. He squeezed her arms before letting go. "One of the few, am I right?"

Robin had been teased about her appearance in junior high: defined cheekbones, thick dark hair, early curves. Coal Queen, they called her. A slur, as though she'd chosen, stupidly, good looks in a place like this. She'd lost the nickname in high school, however, when an actual Coal Queen was crowned from her class. Who was it—Angela Stittman? She'd worn a pageant swimsuit from a department store in Pittsburgh. If Robin had

had the money for the entry fee, she would have been the one crowned. The thought—meaningless—ran unbidden through her head.

"That was a long time ago," she said.

Turning serious, Tom said, "I'm sorry about Ray, honey. I'm glad you came tonight. We're here to help— all of us. Come on over. Sit."

He guided her to a seat by his at the table, next to a stairway that presumably once led to the hotel rooms upstairs. A few strips of yellow hazard tape hung from the banister. Away from the space heater blasting near the barstools, the air was cold. He offered her a chair, and she sat, straightening her shoulders and wishing her sweater had a shallower V.

"Hate to have to say this," Tom said, "but you best put your coat back on. Haven't had a working furnace here since 1983." He poured beer from a pitcher into her glass.

Tom Frost was the one who'd gotten Ray into land-lording to begin with. Ray was interested, toured a few properties, and the Four Points realtor suggested he contact Tom Frost with his questions. The men had hit it off, launching Ray's landlord life. After Ray had died, Tom worked with Scott to collect rent and handle maintenance. No charge for his work or his time. She was grateful. She sipped the beer he poured and almost wept with relief to be beside him. She watched the other arriving landlords carefully. No faces from her past. She tried to relax.

Tom rapped his knuckles on the table. "Listen up," he said.

The men quieted.

"This is Robin Besher. Ray's wife." The men nodded, murmured polite hellos.

Tom pointed at each man as he said, "Ryan Snyder, Gary Greaver, Sam McConnell, Danny Hilson, Jack

Nicholas, Mark Drake. We're on the same side. We're here for you." He turned to the men. "She's taking on Ray's properties. She's one of us."

This got the men's attention. "You local?" asked Mark Drake.

Robin glanced at Tom, who smiled encouragingly. "For now."

"How many's Ray got? Four?"

"Four properties. Seven rental units altogether."

"You think you're up for all that?"

The challenge in his voice nearly made Robin bolt. She didn't want to be up for any part of this.

"I don't have a choice," she said.

"You better listen, honey," Sam McConnell said. "This is hard enough when you been around awhile. You better learn fast. Am I right?"

"When you need tenants, try to find the Marcellus Shale gas workers," Danny Hilson said. "Never had any trouble from them. They won't stay long term, but they'll pay the rent and leave your place in decent shape."

The men leaned forward, watching Robin.

"That's bullshit, Hilson," said Ryan Snyder. "Those guys want nicer places than Ray got. Your best bet is cash up front. That's it. You'll never guess the craziest ones, so get the cash before they move in."

"You'll never know how many people you got living in a place."

"They say someone's sleeping upstairs, that's your signal to not ask questions. Drugs."

"We give them a cheap place to live, they leave us the hell alone. Works both ways."

"Look for bodies in the basement before you buy a place," Ryan Snyder said. "I'm serious. You hear stories. Don't buy nothing blind, even for a deal."

Sam McConnell started laughing.

"Here it comes," said Danny. "Brace yourselves."

"Robin hasn't heard it," Sam said. "I'll be quick." He turned to Robin. "Had this tenant," he said. "Good guy, paid two months up front. Never get that around here. He had this long ass beard, but I thought, whatever. Cash in hand, you know? So he's there, pays his rent on time, don't give me any problems. No police calls, no property destruction, nothing. Easiest money I ever made. Then one day I start getting calls from the neighbor about a lot of noises coming through the walls. 'I'm not trying to make trouble,' she says. 'He's so nice. He's always bringing me eggs in a basket.' This gets my attention, and I tell her I'll talk to him about the noise. No big deal. He's reasonable, right? So I go over to the house and knock on his door. And goddamn if I don't hear a fucking farm inside that place. He ain't home, so I let myself in"—Sam's laughter came from deep in his gut, great wheezes that reddened his face—"and the sonofabitch has chickens in the kitchen cabinets. The doors are off, chicken wire nailed across, chickens inside. Chicken shit and feathers all over the counters and floor. Craziest goddamn thing I ever seen. Had to replace the whole kitchen when I booted him." He wiped his eyes and glanced in Robin's direction. "Honey, there ain't even a moral to that story," he said. "You're in for a wild fucking ride."

"Alright, alright." Tom raised a hand and brought the meeting back around. "We're not trying to scare you, Robin. Every one of us has a story like that. Par for the course when you're running properties."

"You in this long term?" Snyder asked.

"I just want to get my properties in shape, so I can get tenants and raise the rents."

Someone snorted.

"Raise rents?" asked Snyder.

"Yes, probably ten percent mid-year. I just need to renovate two of the properties. I'm living in one of them, and the other is a bigger problem, but—"

The men were talking and laughing over her. Tom banged on the table. "Let's hear her out. Robin, what work do your two places need?"

"The ranch I'm staying in needs some basics—painting, new linoleum, new windows and window coverings, a few new light fixtures. It's pretty grim. The apartment in my triplex has been trashed and needs everything." She turned to Tom. "I was hoping someone might be able to help me figure out where to start."

Tom put a hand on her arm. "We're here for you, Robin."

"Good luck with that," added Snyder. "Getting a full rent roll ain't easy even when you're not renting dumps like Ray's. Forget raising rents. Not that kind of town."

The men looked at her with amusement: a little wife learning a hard lesson about the world.

Tom patted Robin's arm again. "We'll figure it out, okay? You and me."

"Thank you," Robin said quietly. She could barely speak around the lump in her throat. "Ray got some good tenants. I guess I'm lucky."

Tom narrowed his eyes. "You sure these tenants are so different from the rest? You collected rent, what, one time? You get payments from every single tenant?"

"The ones who didn't pay told me—"

"'Ones.' Two out of, what, five? Six? That's rough. You'll have to sort that out. Doesn't matter what they told you. What matters is rent in your pocket. That's the only way it works."

Robin pressed back in her seat like a scolded child.

"I'll give you two pieces of advice, landlord to landlord," he said. "Keep your places filled. That's first. You want to make money, you find tenants. There are always tenants. Second: when shit happens, and it will, do the minimum. Every spritz of 409 is money out of your pocket, you understand?"

Robin nodded. She knew enough not to tell the men she'd spent the day tiling a tenant's bathroom.

"Now, I don't know your whole situation," Tom said. "With Ray gone, I'm assuming these properties are important for you. Call me anytime—I been at this fifteen years, know a lot of people. I'm here to help any way you need."

He clapped once. "Alright, on to business. The Cassatta." A murmur rose. "Let me fill Robin in. You know the building—corner of Ember and Main, the old furniture place? Been slated for demo a couple of years, but the city couldn't hustle the funds. Group called Coketown Investments bought it last month—all-cash offer, formal restoration plan. They made some deal with the city. Now." He paused. "I've got news. Another offer came in last night for the Huron Building—from Coketown Investments."

The men began grousing. Tom rapped his phone on his glass.

"Who told you?" Danny Hilson asked when the din quieted.

"Latshaw," said Tom. "He heard it down at the mayor's office."

"What's the offer?"

"Heard $10K. Basically did the city a favor."

"Who *are* these fucking people?"

"Don't have any details. Sounds serious, though."

"Shit."

Tom glanced at Robin. "The Huron Building was owned by Vic Capelli till this summer. Then something fell off a top floor—what was it, Hilson—a sill? Some glass?"

"A cornice."

"Right. A cornice. And the city took it over, citing safety violations. It's been marked for demo for months, like the Cassatta building was. City couldn't afford to do it." He took a long drink. "Coketown's this generic

DBA. They've got money, though. That plan for the Cassatta is all about historical accuracy, original details, yadda. Safe to say they plan something similar for the Huron. They get these places for nothing and spend a fortune on the renovations. Mayor practically handed the Cassatta over, trying to get it off the city's books. They needed $5K, maybe $6K to tear it down. Coketown comes in, negotiates some secret deal with Videllia, and who the hell knows what they'll do with it?"

"We should run 'em out," Hilson said.

"Town is full of places like the Cassatta," Tom told Robin. "'Good bones.' 'Historical value.' 'Gems of the old Four Points.'"

"My ass," Ryan Snyder said.

Tom went on. "You know what happens when someone starts fixing a place up? Everything around it looks shabbier. And the pressure builds to fix up those places too. It's a snowball. An expensive fucking snowball." Tom continued, "This Coketown Investments outfit ain't from here. Ain't one of us. Ain't no good coming from them, I'm telling you. Speaking of no good, let's talk about Micheline Royer."

The men groaned, rolled their eyes.

"She bought the old Benziger building on Ember Street last month," Tom explained. Robin knew this building: once a drugstore, now an empty storefront next to the Catholic Charities thrift shop.

"Can't do much with a piece of shit commercial property," said Danny Hilson.

"All I'm saying is, last thing we need is Micheline working with Coketown. You know Micheline: once she gets something in her head, you can't shut her up." Tom turned to Robin. "You'll meet her, maybe next meeting. Look. None of us is saying Micheline's a bad person. She gets crazy ideas, though. She wants to do an art gallery."

Uneasily, Robin found herself agreeing with the men. Historically accurate renovations and reducing property blight were ideas she'd supported in Mount Rynda, where she'd chaired a committee that was fundraising to restore a drugstore façade on the north side of town. But Mount Rynda deserved beautiful structures—Four Points deserved nothing. Anyone investing money here was wasting their time and threatening Robin's own tenuous livelihood. The landlords knew best.

Finally, the meeting ended. The men put on their coats, exchanged goodbyes, tossed bills on the table. Tom put his hand on Robin's when she took out her wallet.

"Forget it," he said. "Glad you came. You'll be alright—keep your head above water, that's all."

"Not so easy. The work these places need is crazy."

Tom frowned. "I have to tell you—you're thinking about this the wrong way. Ray never planned to turn his places into the Ritz. That's not the game. The game is easy money. You manage right, you'll get some cash in your pocket. You'll see how it works." He squeezed her arm. "You might even get out of town like you want to."

Robin followed a group of men out. When she reached her car, she realized Danny Hilson was behind her. He lingered by her bumper as she unlocked the door.

"Wanted to ask you," he said, his hands in his pockets. His plaid flannel coat hung open despite the freezing night. "You ain't always been Besher, right?"

"That's my married name."

"What was you before?"

Robin pulled open her door and didn't answer.

"I'm talkin' to you."

Robin slid her right leg into the car. "I was Robin Nowak."

"What I thought," Danny said. "We met before, you and me."

"I don't think so."

"A guy could get insulted," he said. "Liked me alright back then. Now look at you—Mount Rynda. Bet you think you're too good for us. I could tell some stories, though."

A few people exited the Way Car, laughing, their boots crunching the gravel in the lot.

"What do you want?" she said.

Danny laughed. "Sorry to say I'm done with all that. Got a wife at home. Just wanted to say hey," he said. "You and me, we're the kind of people make up this town."

"I haven't lived here for twenty years," Robin said.

Danny leaned over her door and smiled into her face. "Don't matter," he said. "People like us, we always end up right back here."

*   *   *

Robin drove down Water Street, keeping her eyes straight ahead, then turned onto Ember, away from the river, to follow the familiar way home. She still knew these roads. Even after twenty years, she wasn't different. Mount Rynda hadn't erased the giant red sign that seemed to glow on her forehead, a sign that only men in this town could see. They knew they could ruin her and move on with their lives.

People like us, Danny said. Robin chafed against being grouped together but knew all too well the danger of believing she was different. Even as a teenager, she'd felt set apart somehow, and this was what had drawn her to Vincent Latimer. Trevor's father.

Robin met Vincent when she was seventeen on a slow Tuesday night at the Rowdy Buck. She was working in the basement with Cindy by then but kept waitressing part time for plausible deniability. As if anyone believed she was making rent on two shifts a week.

Vincent was sitting at the bar, drinking a Yuengling and blatantly watching Robin run to and from the kitchen. After delivering a plate of jalapeno poppers, she reached over the bar for the plastic cup of water she kept beside the lemons and limes.

"Let me buy you a drink," Vincent said.

She gave her practiced waitress smile. "I'm fine."

He drank another beer, kept watching her. Asked her name and gave his. He stayed at the bar until the end of Robin's shift, then walked her to her car. He was in his forties, wearing a blazer and leather shoes—so different from the men she'd come to know that Robin instantly trusted him.

"I'm in town for work until Friday," he said, leaning into her open window. "Maybe I can see you again. Dinner tomorrow?"

"Dinner."

"A date."

"You're married." The thick gold band was obvious.

"Jealous?"

Most men made excuses, claimed imminent separations or far-fetched marital arrangements. *My wife does her thing, I do mine. I'm married, but I'm not a fanatic about it.*

"Here's their picture," Vincent said, handing her a wallet-size studio shot. Gray-suited, he sat with blond children beside and behind him: two daughters and a son in shades of blue. At his right shoulder, his wife, prim in a shirtwaist dress, her curly blond hair cropped to her chin. The children resembled her. Vincent's face, his features, were nowhere in theirs.

"How old are they?" Robin asked.

"Younger than you," Vincent said. "Fifteen, thirteen, and ten."

"Not so much younger."

He waved dismissively. "They have no idea about the world. Put them out in the wild, and they wouldn't survive one day. They're helpless. And you—" He waited until she met his eye. "You're strong."

In a bathroom stall after her shift the next day, Robin changed into a pale yellow tank top, a short black skirt, black sandals that made assertive *fwap fwaps* as she strode across the restaurant toward Vincent, who was waiting in a booth near the bar.

"I ordered for us," he said. He ran a finger over her knuckles. "Now tell me something: why've you stayed in Four Points?"

Something about how he asked the question made her pause. Usually the question was, *What's a gorgeous girl like you doing in a place like this?* This was something much more probing.

"I've been here my whole life," Robin said. "Not a lot of people come through. Why do you?"

Vincent slid his beer bottle from hand to hand and told her about the mining project he was managing. Their food arrived—steak sandwiches, salads instead of fries—and he told her about his home in Washington, D.C. Robin didn't say much, finding that she liked the sound of his voice. When the check came, Vincent paid, even though Robin could have gotten an employee discount.

"I'll be honest," he said after he counted out a tip. "You're gorgeous. And smart. I know what I want. Talk more outside?"

"I don't think so."

Even as she spoke, she was following him out the door.

They stopped at the edge of the parking lot. "I'll walk you to your car," he said.

"My stuff's still in the restaurant."

"Alright." Vincent put his hand on the back of her neck, pressing her hair against her throat, and kissed her, feverishly. It lasted only a second.

"I'll be back in town next week," he said when he released her. "I'll see you then."

Vincent did come back a week later, with a room already reserved at the Gleason Motor Lodge off Route 129. At Vincent's request, she told no one.

"Here," he said after their first night together. "I got you this." A necklace—a tiny silver deer on a thin silver chain, surprisingly heavy, with pin-sharp antlers that pinched the skin on her chest.

"I thought of you when I saw it," he said. "Four Points. You know—deer." He secured the delicate clasp behind her neck. "You're different from other girls," he said. "You don't belong here."

He'd picked the right poison. She was done for.

He was in Four Points half of each week, nosing around for strip-mining opportunities in the Appalachian foothills. He returned to D.C. on the eight o'clock train every Thursday morning, was back with his family by Thursday afternoon—unless another meeting was scheduled, last minute, for Friday morning. For a year, that "other meeting" was Robin. They always met at the Gleason, in a rear-facing room. She never took money—it wasn't like that, she loved him—but he gave her expensive purses in silk-handled shopping bags, gold jewelry. There were a few dresses without tags, from his wife's closet perhaps, that he liked to fuck her in, the skirt hiked around her waist, the shoulders and sleeves settling unevenly, meant for some other woman's body.

He always said the same things: She was different. Special, powerful. She was destined for bigger places, a bigger life. He never suggested he was the one to provide it, though he was proof that a world beyond Four Points existed, an easy Amtrak ride away.

During the year of their affair, she never took the deer necklace off. The antlers drew blood a few times, when the charm caught under her purse strap or pressed into her throat under Vincent's weight. The punctures pinked and healed and scarred. And Robin became the girl who had been chosen by a reckless, faraway man, so in this way, too, he gave her something worth keeping: a glimpse, a shadow, an unformed but powerful thought that something different was possible.

Decades later, packing to leave Mount Rynda, she'd found the necklace in her bureau. She'd held the charm up to her dim bedroom light, squeezed its tiny, pin-sharp antlers. Without understanding why, she'd put it on.

CHAPTER 5

At four the next afternoon, Robin drove back to 1118 ½ to collect Anne Sackett's delinquent rent. She was desperate. She had to get the money. Anne was in violation of her lease, and Robin was in the legal right here. That didn't change the mortifying fact that she had to chase the money down.

She couldn't bear the idea of hounding a nun. She'd focus on Anne.

Robin knocked and waited, knocked and waited. She went around back to peek in the kitchen windows—where she saw the faucet running, water gushing over the lip of the stopped-up sink.

She sprinted to the front and let herself in. The floor from the kitchen into the living room was flooded. The linoleum in the kitchen was curling at the corners. The living room rug squelched under her shoes.

"Oh shit. Oh shit—" She raced to the kitchen, splashed through a quarter-inch of water to get to the sink, and shoved the faucet closed.

With the water off, the apartment was quiet. She kicked away a few sodden pieces of trash—paper towels, toilet paper rolls. Only then did Robin register what Anne had done to the countertops. Every inch

of Formica was covered in junk—shower caps, plastic
forks and spoons, Diet Coke cans, bottle caps, empty
milk jugs, countless plastic combs in every color of the
rainbow. Robin tried to work free a comb, breaking off
its pink handle. Everything was super-glued.

All other evidence of Anne was gone. No pictures on
the wall, no furniture in the living room. She'd planned
to leave.

Why did Anne hate her? She'd brought her combs.
She'd expressed sorrow over Ray's death. Robin slowly
understood: Ray. Anne hated Ray, not her. Who could
say why. Robin was too defeated to care. Maybe he let
the pipes leak. Maybe he kept the heat too low. Maybe
he was screwing her, which seemed insane but somehow, with water sloshing out of the sink, anything
seemed possible.

Through the thin dividing wall, Robin heard Sister
Eileen moving around. Had she known Anne was leaving? Had she watched her load a truck, drive away?
Was water, at this moment, seeping into her living
room? If it wasn't, it would be soon, killing another
month's rent.

She said a prayer of thanks after finding a broom in
the kitchen closet, and she swept most of the standing
water out the back door. She plunged her hands into the
frigid water to yank the rags out of the drain and emptied the sink. She cracked open the windows, though
the air was too cold to help much. Then she stood there,
in the middle of the wet kitchen floor, cold water creep-
ing through the seams in her shoes. In Mount Rynda,
she'd been a capable person—able to manage a home,
raise a child, organize fancy events. Now she was helpless, as if she'd been dropped naked into the wilderness
and told, simply, *Survive.*

She called Scott Chatham, but it went straight to
voicemail. His calm recorded voice (*You've reached the*

office of Scott Chatham) barely touched her. How could he have helped, anyway?

She called Tom Frost.

"Be there in ten," he said.

From Anne's window, Robin watched him pull up in a Range Rover, as out of place in Four Points as a limousine. He spotted her from the porch and gave a half wave before she opened the door.

He put an arm around her, gave her a squeeze. "Sorry you have to do this on your own. I'm glad you called. You okay?"

She shook her head.

"Alright. It's alright, Robin. Let's just see what we're dealing with."

That *we*, that suggestion of shared determination, brought Robin back to herself. She nodded, too grateful to speak.

When they entered the apartment, Tom gave a low, terrible whistle. He set down his tool box and strode across the sodden carpet, his boots leaving soggy prints.

"I'm so sorry to call with this," she said as she followed him to the kitchen. "I have no idea what to do here. And I can't afford to leave it empty."

Tom's attention was on the countertop. "Have to say, it's a first for me, the super-glued junk." He snorted. "These fucking people." He thumbed at the teeth of a bright blue comb. "It's all gotta come out. Even if you could scrape it off, you'd strip the Formica. This lady knew what she was doing. Any idea why she did it?"

"None. She seemed perfectly nice. I think she must've had some issue with Ray."

"Well, we'll never know," he said. "Might not be any reason. Some people are plain batshit crazy."

"What do I do, Tom? I need a tenant."

"Don't wait on the listing," he said. "Get it into the paper tomorrow, post to the rental boards. Let the calls go to voicemail till you're ready. Trust me, I've seen worse. What you've got is some water damage and some ruined counters." He took a notepad and a Bic from his tool box. "Gonna give you a punchlist," he said. "You follow it, you'll be ready for tenants next week." He dashed off a few notes and tore out the sheet for Robin.

Pull up linoleum
Lay peel-and-sticks
Remove carpet
New carpet by-the-roll
Call Frank Halloran for the counter work

"Schedule Frank for next week," he said. "Tomorrow, pull up the wet shit. Let the floors dry a day or two, then do the tiles and carpet. Done."

"That can't really be all."

"What else are you thinking?"

"Fresh paint, new overhead fixtures—"

Tom lifted his tool box. "I'm gonna stop you right there. You need to understand something. I don't want to scare you," he said, "but you need to come with me."

They drove in his Range Rover a few blocks east, stopping in front of a yellow aluminum-sided triplex. "You sure you're up for this?" he asked grimly.

"I'm ready."

On the outside, the property wasn't the worst Robin had encountered. The siding was bent in places, stained gray at the edges, but the windows weren't broken, and the front door was secure. Three black metal mailboxes hung to the left of the door, the tenants' names written in ballpoint pen on pieces of masking tape. A small plastic flower pot filled with dirt suggested someone's care.

As soon as Tom unlocked the door, Robin realized her mistake. It was the smell, first and foremost, a heavy, toxic stench of sewage and rotten meat. Tom had tenants in the two first-floor apartments. Robin had no idea how they could stand it. She welcomed the paper mask Tom handed her.

"Watch out," Tom warned as they began climbing the stairs. He pulled her to the side so that she wouldn't fall into the rotted-out board of the fifth step. The railing had been torn from the wall. Tom unlocked the door at the top of the stairs and propped it open when they went inside the apartment. The smell was so sharp that Robin staggered backward.

Tom opened the room's two windows. The top pane crashed down from the second one, nearly severing Tom's hand.

"Fuck," he muttered. He shoved a piece of scrap wood underneath to hold the window open.

"Tenant was Chastity Bellerman," he said, the mask moving on his face as he talked. "Twenty-eight years old. Notorious for paying a couple months then flaming out. She's a pain, but a couple months' rent is a couple months' rent. She'll live anywhere. Takes the worst places without batting an eye. Anyway, unfortunately for me, she got strung out while she was living here, went off the rails. Didn't pay rent, got her utilities shut off. And she still wouldn't fucking leave."

"She lived here without water or electricity?"

"Yep."

"For how long?"

"Two months I've been trying to evict her. Cops, the whole deal. She didn't care. Had friends bring her food sometimes. When she quit answering her door there was jack shit I could do. Then she OD'd, and I changed the locks while she was in the hospital."

"She overdosed? Is she okay?"

"She's alive, is all I know. She'll be bothering one of us for an apartment again one of these days."

"This is a horrible story."

"It is a horrible story. Come on—let's see what two months of no water and electric can do." He stamped his foot suddenly with a sickening crunch. Roaches skittered across the filthy floor and walls, scattering into the crevices of peeling paint and cracked plaster.

Robin forced herself to follow him. The bathroom was rank, the shower and sink full of black mold, the toilet thick with sewage. Tom pointed to a gallon jug by the sink.

"Probably filled it at a friend's and flushed with it," he said. "Or tried. C'mon. Kitchen's worse."

He was right. Roaches were everywhere, encrusting the remains of unidentifiable food on the counter, their antenna wiggling from edges of cupboard doors. Tom strode in and opened the fridge, closed it hard.

"Unsavable," he said. He took a roll of duct tape from his box and taped the fridge door shut, slicing the tape violently with a box cutter. Without another word, they strode out of the apartment, down the stairs, and out the door.

They stood together on the front sidewalk, their masks at their chins. Robin breathed the cold air gratefully, though the smell of the apartment stuck on her clothes and skin.

"It's bad," Tom said simply. "New refrigerator, bug bombs, cleaning—who knows if the tub can be saved. This'll set me back a good seven hundred bucks. Nine, maybe." He considered the house. "Gotta do something about that stair, too, before someone cracks their skull open. Accidents like that make the news."

"Someone will live here? With that smell?"

"Are you kidding? I've lost almost two grand. Two months' nonpayment from Chastity, the shit she left— literally. I need someone in there by the end of the month. Listen. This is what we deal with. You can never predict who'll end up screwing you, but someone will.

There's no room for charity. Don't waste your money on improvements, alright?"

Robin nodded.

"Good. Now, about your place. The water screwed the floors, and the glue screwed the counters. That's it. Floors and counters. The rest, you don't touch."

Robin let out a breath. It was good to have direction, good to know that the crisis could be mitigated.

Tom drove her back to Anne Sackett's house.

"I gotta go," he said, not turning off the car. "Final piece of advice: don't get hung up on specifics once the tenant calls come. Get a month's rent in hand, and get 'em moved in. Hang in there, honey. You can do this."

Once Tom's car was out of sight, Robin left too. Tom had made the work sound manageable, but she couldn't know what tomorrow would bring. She didn't have time to panic—she needed new tenants by the start of next week to avoid falling off a financial cliff.

Later, as Robin showered under the hottest water she could stand, she thought about Chastity Bellerman in that apartment. There was a moral to what Tom showed her today, the very opposite of what she taught her own child, but one she'd have to live by if she wanted to survive in a world that had no room for trust, its only promise the one that came with cash delivered on time. Believing anything else would bring disaster to her and Haley. Robin tried to stiffen her spine, square her shoulders, but the day had taken its toll. She slumped into the steam.

CHAPTER 6

The next morning, Robin pulled out her laptop and stared at the cursor blinking in the YouTube search box. *How to remove old linoleum*, she typed. She was stealing Wi-Fi from a neighbor's unsecured account, forcing her request into the ether though she had only two tiny bars of connection. A list of 543 videos appeared after the wait. She clicked on the one with the most views, "Carl's Carpentry: Linoleum Tutorial," stunned that 500,00 people had found reason to watch. Carl was brawny and bald and good with his hands. He was wearing a red bandanna over his head and, oddly, white socks and no shoes. Calm and serious, with no inclination to chit-chat with his viewers, he laid out the required tools and got to work.

Robin watched all ten minutes of the video. When the video began a second time, Haley appeared at Robin's shoulder and leaned over to watch too before leaving for the bus.

"Doesn't seem too hard," she said.

"Doesn't it?"

"Get that buzzing thing he has. Seems pretty important."

The buzzing thing was a Ridgid JobMax 12-Volt Multi-Tool, which Robin bought at Home Depot for a breathtaking $99. She also bought black trash bags and a bulk-size box of rubber gloves. Ray's tool box held a box cutter and a scatter of new blades. She wore old yoga pants and a sweat-stained tank she'd worn out doing Bikram classes in Mount Rynda.

Robin sat on the grimy floor and tugged at the first curled corner, closest to the drafty back door, then scored the linoleum in a grid as far as she could stretch. She peeled off the gloves so she could hold her tools and the damp, slimy linoleum more firmly, pushing away her disgust. She didn't have time for that. The filth couldn't be scrubbed out. She had to look past it if she was going to get anything done.

From her iPhone's radio, Garth Brooks was singing about summers and wheat fields. As she loosened the linoleum with the buzzing tool, the soggy old glue dissolved into a gooey brown puddle. A pile of linoleum scraps began to grow behind her. Gray, foamy filth lodged under her nails. What would Kim—her old manicurist—say if Robin sat at her station, her usual Va-Va Vino nail color long gone? Robin pushed her fingers under a tile for more leverage and split the nail on her index finger down to the quick.

She bagged the scraps and shoved the bags into the trunk of her car. Then she mixed bleach and warm water in a bucket and mopped the raw floorboards until the room blurred.

Taking a break outside, she breathed deeply, icy air mingling with bleach fumes in her mouth and nose. Nettle Street was quiet in the middle of the day. Robin was utterly alone, on this block, in Four Points. Tom Frost was willing to offer advice and expertise, but he wasn't her husband. He wouldn't offer spare supplies or spend all day tearing up linoleum. She and Haley were on their own. She rubbed her cold arms with damp, pruned fingers, shivering. This wasn't the first time she'd kept herself afloat in Four Points, and she felt a thin simmer of pride. She could acknowledge, without panicking, that whatever help she might be offered would never be enough.

A memory flashed: Vincent. The version of help he'd attempted. The first time he brought groceries to their motel room, he'd seemed surprised by how grateful she was. Two packages of Fudge Stripe cookies, a box of saltines, a few cans of soup, a loaf of bread—an afterthought as he bought his own lunch. Her gratitude had been impossible to conceal as she recalculated that week's expenses in her head. His expression had been quick but piercing—he hadn't realized until that moment the difference he could make.

After that, he'd brought fruits and greens and cereal and bread. Juice, boxed dinners, rice she could boil in the bag. Treats too—cookies and candy—as though she were a child. In the dead of winter, when her cough had kept them both awake, he went to Thrift Drug in the morning for cough medicine and Tylenol. He'd been hesitant, that day, to leave her.

One day he'd asked how she paid her rent when she waitressed only two shifts a week.

"Other ways of making money around here," she'd said.

"Are you selling drugs?"

She shook her head. And then he knew.

He began giving her cash along with the groceries. "I'm not paying you," he'd said bluntly, handing over the first few twenties. "Do you understand me? I want to be clear. I'm not one of those guys. This is different."

She'd gone along, though sex plus money was a familiar equation. The difference lay somewhere in those bags of groceries, in the cough medicine. The money had made her feel cared for, protected.

Robin shook her head, breathed the cold air deeply again. What Vincent had given wasn't *help*. He'd taken what he'd wanted and risked nothing in return. He hadn't had to fear discovery or worry she'd try to follow him. He was simply passing through, confident that Four Points would always be right where he left it. No need to look back.

She'd let him play the savior. She'd needed so much more.

Robin spent the rest of the week undoing Anne's damage piece by piece. While the kitchen floor dried, she ripped up the living room rug, removing the staples with a screwdriver. The rug was wet from the flooding. Mold spores bloomed in black patches, which she tried to avoid as she rolled the carpet into a thick, unwieldy tube.

When the floors were dry, she spent a day laying brick-patterned peel-and-stick tiles in the kitchen, cutting them to fit with a box cutter when she reached a wall or cabinet. In the living room, she installed new carpeting, low-pile indoor/outdoor she'd bought by the foot from Home Depot. Haley rode her bike over after school to help. She stood on the new rug to keep it straight while Robin moved along the edge with a staple gun.

"Can I try?" Haley said.

Robin hesitated. The staple gun made a threatening *bang* each time she shot a staple into the floor. But then, when was the last time Haley had expressed interest in anything new?

"Just make sure you point it down," Robin said.

Haley rolled her eyes and took over the stapling in Robin's stead. She was confident, quick, her arm strong against the whoosh of the stapler. Her father's daughter. He'd probably shown her how.

"Okay," Robin said. "What's wrong?"

Haley shrugged, but her despair was obvious in her downturned mouth and the purposeful way she stared at the floor as she shot staples from the gun.

"Amber still bothering you?"

"She wrote some stuff about me on a group text," Haley said. "None of it's true, but everyone believes it. At least they're pretending to."

"You're part of a group text?"

"*Mom*. No. It's all Amber's friends."

Robin was too tired to ask for details. She put her hand on Haley's cheek. "Tomorrow she'll be after someone else. You know that."

"I heard it might be Daisy."

"Good."

Robin hated this girl. Amber was so purely mean—a true product of Four Points. The sooner they could get away from these people, the better.

On her sixth and last day of work at 1118 ½, Robin painted the doorway and window trim in the kitchen. She didn't scrape, and she did it backward, after the new floor instead of before, but she wanted to do it despite Tom Frost's advice. It was an invisible rebellion. She was pleased that she'd made the apartment almost nice. Someone might actually want to live here.

She stood too quickly when she finished the last of the trim, and blood rushed from her head. She reached out to steady herself, pressing both hands against the shiny, wet paint. The prints on the gloss showed every ridge. She smeared her prints with a slick of paint. When she stepped back to assess, she could still see them, thin and breathy.

She cleaned the brushes with turpentine and wrapped the paint-heavy foam roller heads in newspaper. Paint stuck stubbornly along the edges of her fingers. When she rubbed it with her thumbs, it peeled away like skin.

A rare sense of satisfaction, of completion, settled over her as she drove home. Tonight, the paint would dry, and in the morning the apartment would be whole. Not new, not beautiful, but ready to live in. And she'd done it with her own two hands. Her skin itched, dry and flaking from the labor.

* * *

There was only one voicemail. One single, unpromising voicemail in response to the ad she'd placed for Anne's apartment. A woman, who said, "Calling 'bout the listing," and gave a phone number. No one answered when Robin returned the call, but she left a message inviting the woman to visit the property at four that afternoon.

Unsure if anyone would show up, Robin arrived early to turn on the lights and wipe the new countertops. She waited anxiously by the front window. It didn't matter who came—as long as they left a first month's rent behind. She would not ask any questions. She needed this woman, whoever she was, to say yes.

A beat-up Camry pulled to a stop in front of the duplex. Robin smoothed her hair, plucked a piece of brown leaf from the carpet. She stood and looked out the window once more.

"Oh my God," she said. The voice on the message had been so ordinary, a local woman making apartment-hunting calls. But it wasn't just any local woman coming up the walk. It was Cindy Sweeney, more than twenty years a stranger.

Cindy was on the porch, preparing to knock. She wore makeup that was too dark for her complexion. She had long, fried hair. Hair that would be just as sticky and stiff as it'd been all those years ago if Robin were to touch it. She was big—tall, big breasts, big bones—and she filled the space around her in a way that seemed to dare Robin to tell her to step aside. Cornered, Robin froze. She wanted to deadbolt the door and run out the back, but she couldn't. Winter was a bad time to hunt for tenants, and the possibility of 1118 ½ sitting empty until spring was very real. Robin did what she had to. When Cindy knocked, Robin opened the door.

There was a flash of surprise and immediate recognition. "Robin fucking Nowak," Cindy said.

"Besher now."

"Right. Ray Besher. Your moneybags husband. Heard about that."

"Ray's dead."

She said it without thinking, the words rousing challenge, even triumph. *You think you know me? You don't know anything.*

Cindy squinted, appraising. "That why you're back?"

"You think I'd be here if I had a choice?"

Cindy dismissed the question with no more than a loud exhalation. "So this place is yours."

"I'm getting some things in order before going back to Mount Rynda."

"You too good for us?"

Robin was freezing by the open door. "You still want to look around?"

"I'm here, ain't I?"

Neither woman spoke as Robin led Cindy through the living room and into the kitchen. With new carpet, tiles, and counters, both downstairs rooms were nicer than most Four Points rentals, but Cindy made no comment. Upstairs, the two small bedrooms were in worse shape: stained beige shag carpet, crooked window blinds, bare bulbs. With three strides, they were in the bathroom at the end of the hall. Discolored bathtub, no shower. An old white porcelain sink over exposed plumbing.

"This place is a shithole," Cindy announced.

Back downstairs, they stood under the harsh overhead in the living room.

"It'll be me and Amber moving in here," Cindy said. "Keep to ourselves, pretty much. You won't have a problem with us."

"Amber?"

"My daughter. Thirteen. Eighth grade at Sacred Heart."

Of course Haley's tormenter was Cindy Sweeney's daughter. Robin almost laughed out loud.

"I really don't think—"

Cindy cut her off. "I'll be straight with you," she said. She draped her long ponytail over a shoulder and twisted the ends around her fingers. "I'm in a bad situation, okay? Trying to get out and start over. I don't have a lot of choices here. You as my landlord? That's bullshit. Fuck it. Fuck you too. This is what it is."

"Someone else came by already," Robin said. She smelled cigarette smoke when Cindy scoffed. "And you're a smoker. It's a nonsmoking property."

For a long moment, Cindy looked at her, and Robin looked back. Mascara-clumped lashes, pockmarked cheeks, the skin across her collarbone wrinkled and limp, old before its time. The *yinzes*, the *ain'ts*, the *fucks*. If Robin closed her eyes, she'd see sixteen-year-old Cindy, the coin-flip side of this woman standing in the living room. Against all odds, she needed something from Cindy Sweeney: her money, what little there was, and her assurance that, under her watch, nothing calamitous would happen to this apartment. There were other people, surely. If Robin waited long enough, she'd find someone else. But she couldn't wait.

Cindy rustled through her purse. "Here's the first month," she said. "Four hundred. You want to count it?" She extended a secondhand envelope from a credit card bill, the jagged flap resealed with a piece of scotch tape. Robin shoved it into her pocket.

"Cindy."

"Yeah?"

"There's a nun next door."

"She won't bother me."

"She'll know who's coming and going."

"So?"

"I don't want her to be—uncomfortable."

Cindy took one step closer to Robin. "I work at Walmart," she said. "Got it? That's what I do. I work the fucking register. Sometimes I work all fucking night because we're open twenty-four fucking hours. You want my nametag? A pay stub? My timesheet for the shifts I pull while you're sleeping like a goddamn princess?"

"I just had to say something."

"You just had to say something. Bet you've been waiting to say something for a long fucking time."

A moment passed. Robin asked quietly, "Do you know who lives in that house now?" Every memory she had of Cindy was wrapped in that basement. That hulking specter on Whistlestop Road.

"Hell no," Cindy said. "You should drive by now you're back." She turned to the door. "We're the same, you and me," she said over her shoulder. "I'm a 'team member' at Walmart, you're a fucking slumlord. A fucking *slumlady*. Don't worry about the nun. Nuns love people like us. They have to love the sinners the most."

The door was too hollow and cheap to properly slam.

*   *   *

It was fully dark at 4:30 p.m. when Robin left Nettle Street. Even though Haley was waiting at home, Robin skipped the turn that led to their rental and wound toward the river, to the house on Whistlestop Road she used to share with the Sweeneys. She turned onto the street as though under a spell.

Whistlestop Road was a dead end and a hill street, set high above the river and the west side of town, accessible by the winding artery of Ember Street or by one of the steep, narrow staircases linking these high upper streets to the railroad tracks on Water Street below. Through the darkness, Robin could make out the stone wall that split, spilling into the narrow steps. If she walked to the precipice, she'd be able to hear the Yough, frosted thickly with ice now but never still.

Don't fall in, Robin used to tell Cindy, a blackout drunk long before she had a legal ID.

That river, always threatening to take someone. And all Robin had done was move a little ways downstream.

Past two boxy, unkempt houses and a prefab ranch with a collapsing side deck stood the house she sought, the last on the left. Three stories of dirty red brick, two windows sloppily boarded on the second floor, the attic windows missing entirely. A large, bowed picture window, a hole shot through the right-hand pane, over-looked a wraparound porch littered with broken bricks, cracked cement, and pieces of old wooden railings. The second-floor bedroom windows looked down onto train tracks. In the fall, the turret window revealed a sea of red and gold, the tracks and the Youghiogheny River winding through in ribbons of bronze and onyx. On the front door fluttered a white notice: CONDEMNED.

Impulsively, Robin turned off the car and stared at the house: larger than she remembered, farther away from the neighbors. The extent of disrepair was sur-prising. It had always been shabby inside, unabashedly dirty, full of furniture scavenged curbside on trash day. The paint had been peeling, the hardwood floors had creaked and cracked, and the rattling wooden windows had let in every icy gust. The house had been rough but not wrecked like it was now, the windowpanes not shot or shattered.

Robin saw herself: sixteen, climbing out of her beat-up white Mazda, indigo-black hair loose to her waist, slouching up to the porch where Rochelle would push open the screen door and say, "Cindy's in the basement. Go on down." Twenty-seven years ago. As clear as yesterday.

Robin remembered too well what went on in that basement. But she wasn't willing to revisit what had happened in one of the rooms upstairs, the room where her son had slept. Memories of the sex work—when they arrived, unbidden—nauseated her. Thoughts of Trevor stopped her breathing.

Wind gusted. A shingle from the roof cartwheeled to the ground. She tasted blood. She'd bitten through the skin behind her lower lip. It hurt, but she kept the broken bulb of chewed skin between her teeth.

As she started the car and moved her hands to the steering wheel, her left elbow hit the lock button, firing a quick loud crack. The noise roused dogs in the house across the yard. Two tall black Dobermans threw themselves at the fence, jumping and barking, straining against the strips of blue tarp woven through the chain link.

A light flickered in the kitchen window of the old house, weak as a candle flame. Nothing but a nervous illusion—the reflection of a star. Robin K-turned the car and left the house behind.

CHAPTER 7

On Monday, as Haley was hoisting her backpack over her coat, a piece of toast between her teeth, Robin told her.

"I don't want you to worry about it," Robin began, "but I rented 1118 ½ to Amber Sweeney and her mom. If she's meaner than usual, this could be why."

"She's the tenant? Like, paying us?" Haley said.

"That's right."

"We need Amber's *money*?"

"You can't look at it that way. We need the income from the apartment—it doesn't matter who lives there. This is landlording, honey. As long as I have tenants in the properties, everything works."

"Did Dad always have tenants?"

"Your dad had an eye for people." Haley didn't need to know this wasn't exactly true.

"Would he have let the Sweeneys in?"

"If he had to, yes. This is our livelihood. I can't afford any more losses."

"Dad would never do this to me."

"I'm doing it *for* you, Haley. For us." She stopped herself. Took a breath. "Go on. You'll miss the bus."

Haley ran out the door.

Robin had no business sending Haley to Sacred Heart. In Mount Rynda, Haley's tuition at Our Lady was deducted automatically from checking, and Robin thought no more about it than she did about gravity keeping her rooted to the earth. Now, parochial school was an unjustifiable luxury. Robin applied for and was granted financial aid—the death of a parent guaranteed it—and today she brought her reduced check to Sacred Heart. Signing her name on the aid sheets, while the secretary watched with a blank face, was humiliating. But she would do this one good thing for Haley—the only thing she could.

After paying tuition, Robin drove to Walmart determined to complete her distasteful errands by the time Haley got home. She filed in with the relentless Walmart crowds, hating that she relied so much on the markdowns. She worried about a run-in with Cindy Sweeney, but a careful scan of the lanes showed that Cindy wasn't working the registers. So she was horrified when she heard Cindy's voice over her shoulder in the checkout line.

"Fancy meeting you here," Cindy said.

In the overheated store, Robin clearly smelled Cindy's cigarette smoke and the chemical sweetness of her hairspray.

"Cindy," Robin said. With Cindy behind her, a rack of magazines to her right, three bins of gum and candy bars to her left, she had no escape from the lane. "How's the apartment?"

Cindy blew her bangs out of her eyes. "It's fine. Clyde's giving me shit about taking my furniture, but we'll be alright. Cheap shit anyway." A new look crossed her face: curiosity. "Never seen you here. You coming from somewhere else?"

"Paying tuition at the school." She knew her mistake immediately.

"Paying in person? What—you on aid?"

Lying was pointless. "Yes."

"Thought my rent was paying Haley's way."

"Of course not."

"Where's that money going?"

Blood rushed into her ears. "Maintaining the prop-erties is expensive," she said. She felt an urgent push to make Cindy understand—what it cost, why she was here. "Damages, repairs, vacancies. But I'll keep Haley in that school as long as we're here. I'll give up anything but that."

"So charge more rent."

"I can't."

"Not when you rent to people like me, right?" Cindy hacked out a laugh and shook her head. "Think you're so much better than me. My credit's good, you know that? I work hard. I could live somewhere better. I could put something down for my own place. I need your cheap ass rent so I can afford to send Amber to Sacred fucking Heart." She casually took out a tube of magenta lipstick and colored her lips, examining Robin's cart. "Still with the cashews, huh?"

"Ray ate them."

"Bullshit. You were eating cashews when we were fifteen."

"I doubt that."

"That's fucking hilarious. There was a gumball machine out at that bar by the highway, full of fancy nuts. One with actual gumballs, one with cashews. You used to pop quarters in there nonstop."

"Okay. Whatever. I'm not going to fight about this."

Cindy scoffed and checked her phone.

Robin didn't believe her. She'd bought cashews for Ray from the Whole Foods bulk aisle, tied her bags of organic nuts and beans and dried fruits with little white flags, the bin number marked with a chained-up ballpoint pen. When she paused to consider, though, she remembered something else: the cold knob twisting between her fingers, the *ka-chunk* of the dropping quarter, nuts tumbling into her palm from the dangling silver hatch. A joke, cashews with cheap beer in a dive bar. Robin shook it off. What did it matter, when she started eating cashews? She willed the line forward.

Three people ahead. A woman with a circular from Shop 'n Save was haggling over the price of canned peaches. She had ten cans on the belt—more canned peaches than Robin had eaten in her life. The light above the register was flashing; a manager had been called. Everyone stood and waited.

"Fucking price-match promise," Cindy muttered. Then she leaned in and said in a low voice, "Hold on. Nine o'clock. Now look at that guy."

Robin looked over. A man in lane five was loading a stack of huge gray plastic storage bins onto the conveyor. He was wearing a camouflage baseball hat and coat, gray sweatpants, and muddy Timberlands. Once the bins were scanned and paid for, he hoisted them into his arms in a show-offy way and kicked his cart into the middle of the aisle.

Robin watched him walk away. "That's a lot of bins," she said.

"You don't know who that was?" Cindy coughed out a laugh when Robin shook her head. "Your memory ain't too good."

The woman with the peaches resolved her problems and lumbered out of the store with her heavy plastic bags. The line finally moved forward a few paces.

"You should know that guy," Cindy pressed.

"Well, I don't."

"Fred Strempek."

"Who?" Robin had to think only a moment before she knew. "*Him?*"

"Him," Cindy said smugly. She nodded with a small, closed-lip smile, pleased to have shocked Robin.

"Wasn't he—"

"In jail, yeah, but just for some outstanding fines. They never got him for anything else."

"Were they supposed to?"

"Who the hell knows?" Cindy leaned in again, too close. "Probably be pretty happy if you said hi next time you see him."

"That's not going to happen."

"You have a lot in common. He bought a couple trailers in Laurel Estates. You can talk tenants." She paused. "And old times."

Sweating, Robin unzipped her polar fleece and loosened her scarf. Her toes were overheating in her snow boots. She was finally close enough to the register to unload her cart, and her purchases traveled down the conveyor, closer to freedom than she was.

Cindy hoisted her shopping basket onto the child seat of Robin's cart while Robin waited to pay. Cindy rested her arms on top and leaned over, like she had all the time in the world.

"Saw Andy Gilligan here last week," she said. "Came right through my line. 'Hey, Cin,' he says, like we're old friends. 'How's it goin',' he says, and I says, 'It's fine,' and he says, 'You still at the Estates?' and I says, 'I got a new place in town,' and he says—"

"Sixty-four thirty-seven," the cashier said to Robin. Cindy kept talking while Robin counted out exact bills and change and piled her bags back into the shopping cart.

"—He pulls out his fucking wallet and says, 'Andy Jr. made varsity' and shows me a picture of this Mini Andy with a bat over his shoulder, like I care about this kid, and I says—"

"Cindy."

"—I says—"

"Cindy. *Shut up.*" Robin's voice carried from her lane, lane three, easily to lane twelve, over the heads of teenage girls and housewives and barn-coated men with their ponytails pulled through mesh caps. She grabbed Cindy's basket out of her cart and slammed it onto the conveyor.

"What the *fuck*?" Cindy said, pulling her shoulders back.

"Leave me alone," Robin said. "I don't care about this. I don't want to hear about this. I just want to get the hell out of here."

An unimaginable possibility flashed through Robin's mind—a fight in lane three, Cindy pummeling her on the dirty tile, Robin cowering as the rest of Four Points cheered them on. She put a hand to her forehead, rubbed her temples, fought dizziness. She could hear a younger Cindy saying, *You want Robin or me?* and then, fearfully, *Robin, I'm calling an ambulance, something's wrong with him.* Her vision blackening, Robin pushed her cart out of the store, across the parking lot, into an empty space next to her car. She leaned on the cart until she was sure she wouldn't faint and put her bags into the trunk.

She took a few painful breaths while the engine struggled to warm. The men Cindy mentioned—the names she tossed around like snowballs, bright and harmless—were, to Robin, savage ghosts from her past, newly risen from the dead. Seeing their faces, hearing their names—for Cindy, they were just part of Four Points. They'd always been here, always would be. For twenty years, Robin had lived as though the past had never happened. She'd let herself believe it. But the men had been there all along, only ninety minutes down the road. The cold air pierced her lungs. The world was made of shattered, stabbing glass.

She put the car in gear and backed out of her parking space, then slammed on the brakes. She'd nearly run over Cindy Sweeney, who now stood a few feet back, her arms raised, her *What the fuck?!* audible even from inside the car.

Robin lowered the window. "My God, Cindy, I didn't see you," she said. "Are you okay?"

"I was tapping on your rear fucking window," Cindy said. "What the hell is wrong with you?"

"I was fine until you rented my place," Robin blurted out. "I haven't thought about Fred Strempek since I was seventeen, and there he is, twenty feet from me—"

"I didn't bring this shit to you," Cindy said, not unkindly.

"How can you stand it?" Robin said. "What they did to us. Didn't you ever want to press charges? You chit-chat with them at the store and let them get away with what they did—"

"You think I wanna live that way? My whole life a fucking shit show of revenge?"

"They broke the law. They took advantage. We were kids, Cindy."

"We were kids," Cindy agreed. "We were stupid, we let some really bad shit happen to us. I ain't trying to say they didn't do what you're saying. And I sure as hell ain't saying I asked for it, even though I did. I was seventeen. Who the fuck knows what I wanted? But here's what I want now: my own fucking life. What do you want?"

Robin sighed. "I want to go home."

"Who's stopping you?"

Robin rolled up her window. She reversed again, more carefully. The light was fading, the sky bright and clean with snow clouds. Robin was shaking, barely able to keep her hands steady on the wheel. This was why she'd left. *This was why she'd left.* Unlike Cindy, she'd never be able to live with all of her desperate mistakes. And worse—accepting her past with Cindy meant inviting the rest in too.

Getting back to Mount Rynda was more urgent than ever. With Anne's apartment rented, Robin could devote herself to the East Green wreck, making it habitable, getting a tenant. She had to shut out the distractions, keep her focus on what mattered: leaving Four Points by spring.

Robin was still shaking when she stopped at the light at the base of the Ember Street Bridge. A figure was walking toward her on the sidewalk, clutching a bundle. The light changed. Robin drove past the walker—a young girl, carrying in her arms not groceries but a haphazardly wrapped baby.

Robin was off the road, blinkers on, in seconds. Sharp air stung through the window.

"Can I give you a ride?" Robin called.

The girl glanced over but kept walking.

"Please," Robin said. "It's freezing."

The girl crossed without checking traffic and stood by Robin's window, beyond arm's reach. She was hazel-eyed and unsmiling. No hat, matted mousey hair stuffed into the collar of her oversized tan trench. Her cheeks and nose were pink with cold. Draped around the baby were wide knit scarves, an unbuttoned cardigan sweater, a fleece blanket in Steelers black and gold.

"I was at a friend's," the girl said. "Thought she was driving me home." Her youthful defensiveness reminded Robin instantly of Haley.

Robin unlocked the doors with a click, and the girl climbed in behind Robin. She pressed the baby to her chest when she leaned over to close the door.

"Where do you live?"

"I ain't telling you."

"Where should I take you?"

"Let me out on Burdock."

Robin checked the rearview mirror every few seconds, but the girl never met her eye. She didn't look at the baby either. After a few minutes, she shrugged and shifted and reached inside her coat to adjust her shirt. She was nursing the baby, may have been nursing even as she was walking on the bridge. Keeping the child calm and warm.

"Boy or girl?" Robin asked, glancing again in the mirror.

"Why do you care?"

Robin turned right onto Burdock Street.

"Here's good," the girl said.

"Are you sure? I can take you to your house—I don't care how far it is."

"Here's good."

She pushed open the door before Robin had fully stopped. She slammed the door closed without a word, then rapped a knuckle on Robin's window.

"Thanks for the ride," the girl said. "Wanna see her?" She parted a tangle of wraps and leaned forward. An infant no bigger than a watermelon, her tiny mouth slack against the girl's bare breast, shuddered in the sudden splash of cold. The girl tugged the wraps back into place.

"Later," she said, halfway gone before Robin could say a word.

CHAPTER 8

At two in the morning on Friday, Sister Eileen called about a commotion at 1118 ½.

"I think you better come," she said. "I don't want to call the police."

There was no way to know how long she would have to be gone. Robin rolled over and shook Haley gently.

"Haley. Haley, wake up."

She wrapped a coat around Haley's shoulders as they headed to the car. By the time they got to Nettle Street, Haley was more alert.

"What happened?" she said.

"Not sure. Sister Eileen called."

They were silent as they made the turn, the heater blasting.

Robin pulled to the curb. "Stay here. I'll find out what's going on."

Haley curled in her seat, trying to sleep again. Robin got out of the car and locked the doors. The lights were on throughout the duplex, clearly showing that the downstairs windows on Cindy's side had been broken. Robin heard another splinter and crash from the back of the house, and Cindy's shouting from inside.

"Fucker! Get the fuck out of here, you asshole!"

A scrawny man in jeans and a tank top ran around to the front, a belt in one hand and a beer in the other. When he saw Robin, he hurled the can at the front of the house, jumped into a pickup, and squealed away. For a long moment, Robin heard nothing but the fizzing puddle of beer on the porch. Then Cindy Sweeney yelled, "Fuuuuuccccckkkk!"

Robin knocked on the door, nodded at Cindy when she answered wearing purple plaid boxers and a t-shirt. The living room was a jumble of piled furniture and boxes shoved against the wall. On the couch was Amber, wearing a Hello Kitty bathrobe, her arms around her knees. The living room and kitchen, where Robin had laid new carpet and tile, were full of broken glass.

"Watch yourself," she said, nodding at Cindy's bare feet. "What happened?"

"Finally got my stuff," Cindy said. "Then Clyde came over and smashed the windows. *Shit.*"

She didn't blame, didn't cry, didn't apologize or excuse. Because of this, Robin didn't feel angry. She didn't point out the hundreds of dollars she'd have to spend on new windowpanes, new paint. She didn't howl that these unforeseen expenses were destroying her hope of fixing East Green as soon as possible.

All she said was, "I have some duct tape in my car. You and Amber unpack those boxes. We'll cover the windows with the cardboard. You'll freeze tonight otherwise."

Outside, Sister Eileen was sopping up the beer with paper towels, a plain cotton bathrobe over an ankle-length nightgown and sneakers.

"Sister Eileen," Robin said. "I'm so sorry about this."

Sister Eileen rose. "Can I do anything inside?"

"You've done enough."

"I want to help."

Robin sighed and said, "Alright. Let me get my daughter." When she looked at the car, Haley was awake and gazing back. Robin retrieved the duct tape, and together they walked inside.

Robin and Cindy fitted flattened cardboard boxes jigsaw-style over the windows, and Amber and Haley pressed long strips of duct tape along the edges, cutting the tape with a pair of dull kitchen scissors. Both girls were in their pajamas and robes, with tangled ponytails and tired faces, as though this were a sleepover. Sister Eileen swept the broken glass and vacuumed the floors again and again.

The house was cold when they finished, smelling of damp cardboard. It was almost four in the morning.

"Shouldn't we call the police?" Sister Eileen asked.

Cindy shook her head. "It'll make it worse."

"I saw him take off his belt—his pants nearly fell down," Sister Eileen said. "Not the sharpest knife in the drawer, is he?"

"I should've known," Cindy said. "Two fucking years. Story of my life."

"God has a plan," Sister Eileen began.

Cindy scoffed.

"Even in this. Especially in this." Sister Eileen bowed her head as she walked to the door.

Once the nun was gone, Cindy ushered Amber to bed. When she came back downstairs, she seemed defeated, nothing at all like Cindy.

"I'm sorry," she said in a low voice. "Shit like this is why you didn't want me here, and you're thinking you got proved right. Same old fuck-up Cindy Sweeney. You're wrong, but fuck that. We can be out by next week."

"You don't have to leave," Robin said. "This wasn't your fault."

"It's my fucking mistake. Like always."

"We'll figure out the windows, somehow."

"How?"

"Somehow." Without anything else to offer, Robin turned to leave.

"Robin."

"Yes?"

"Amber's taking this hard."

From behind her, Haley said, "I won't talk about it at school. Amber doesn't have to worry."

They didn't speak on the dark ride home. Robin wanted to touch Haley's cheek but instead kept her hands on the wheel. Robin felt a kind of peace, a kind of thankfulness. All those months of searching and now, here, grace.

CHAPTER 9

Nearly every morning, a text waited from Steph Pachol-ski. Her initial string of worried questions had dwindled to a single heart. Though grateful for the messages, Robin never replied. The thread connecting her to Mount Rynda was fragile, and the blunt force of anything Robin might say about Four Points would sever it cleanly. She deleted each message, a daily ritual of turning away.

That morning, her phone rang as she was deleting the latest of Steph's greetings.

"Robin? Hi, it's Deirdre Boone from 3201 Foxtail. Listen, I hate to call, but I have to tell you—I haven't had hot water for three days."

"Three *days*?"

"Well, at first I thought it was, you know, so cold outside, and I wanted to give it some time. It was tepid—not icy. Now it's icy. I hate to bother you. I waited as long as I could. I really hoped it'd get better on its own."

Her voice was apologetic, but when she stopped talking, the silence was expectant.

"I'm so sorry," Robin said. "I'll come over and take a look." It seemed like the right landlord thing to say.

When she arrived, Deirdre led Robin to the dank, dim cellar. The ceiling was so low she could touch it with her elbow bent. She crouched beside the water heater. Water in a clear glass tube, pipes, valves.

"Is it—on?" she said. She had no idea how water heaters ran.

"I don't think so. I'm not sure, though. If it is, it's not heating anything up."

Robin gingerly touched the main valve with two fingers, turned it experimentally. "Okay. Try it now," she said. Deirdre dutifully went to the kitchen. Robin heard water rushing in the pipes.

A minute later, Deirdre came back. "Sorry, Robin. Ice cold."

"I'll have to get some parts," Robin said. "Mind if I come back later?"

"I'll be at work, so let yourself in. I really appreciate it."

Parts: Was this the right word?

Replacing Anne Sackett's floors and counters cost $550, leaving $2,875 in her shoebox of cash. This small sum stood between her and a full-blown panic attack. She and Haley would not starve. She had to believe this unconditionally. Robin needed to mold the parts out of Play-Doh, form the pieces from melted screws, channel the ghosts of handymen from long ago. She needed to save what money she had for fixing East Green. She couldn't yet face the impact of Cindy's window fiasco.

She called Tom Frost.

*   *   *

It was Robin's property, but after unlocking the door, Tom Frost led the way to the cellar.

"There she is," Tom said, striding to the water heater. "She and I, we've met before." He dinged the heater with his knuckles. "Still a piece of shit." He rummaged a headlamp from his tool box. "Hold this," he said, handing

Robin a wrench. He clanged once more through the box and fished out a pair of pliers, then pulled Robin to a crouch beside him and directed the headlamp onto a tarnished valve. His cologne had a department store smell, rich and anonymous. He tinkered around a little, flicked a tiny flame on and off, replaced the valve with another identical valve.

"She say anything about a strange odor or color?"

"She didn't mention that."

"Could be the anode," he said. "Could be this baby's seen better years." He fiddled with another valve. Finally he said, "Good enough."

"It's fixed?"

"Hell no. It'll work for a little while, at least."

"How much to replace it?"

"You're looking at $700 right off. That's your smallest unit without installation. Don't get crazy."

"But she needs hot water. She waited three days to call."

"She'll have it, and then she won't, and we'll start over, alright?" He put a hand on her back. "Come on. Let's have a talk."

They sat in front of Deirdre's kitchen mural, and Tom poured coffee from a Thermos into two pocked foam cups from his tool box.

"Okay. Why're you doing so much for this tenant?"

"She's a good tenant. Hates to complain."

"She *did* complain."

"Well, yes, but her water—"

Tom waved her off. "She complained, and you jumped to help. That's a mistake." He nodded, breathed in, warmed to his subject. "Around here, you got a lot of people with nothing. They need a place to live, though, and they ain't picky. Four walls and a roof, you know? Basic stuff. You don't need to give a lot of extras. Collect their rent and live your life."

He sipped his coffee, letting his words sink in.

"Stop answering the phone. Next time your hot-water girl calls, send it to voicemail."

"She didn't have hot water!"

"All I'm saying is, it's a slippery slope, the maintenance calls. You gotta set the expectations. You ain't renting penthouses. They understand what they're getting. You want to make money, you listen to what I'm telling you." He reached over the table, patted Robin's hand in a fatherly way. "You're a nice woman, Robin. Too nice. You need to be a little bit more like us."

As she drove home from Deirdre's, she grew more and more certain that Tom was right. She *was* a nice person, a good person, but if she didn't take a harder line, she'd have no hope of getting anywhere—and she needed to get back to Mount Rynda as urgently as she needed to breathe. She didn't have the luxury of thinking about how to make things better.

*   *   *

By four in the afternoon, Robin felt a deep weariness that had little to do with the hour. If she sat down—on the couch, on the floor—she'd sleep for a hundred years. She stayed standing. The closing music from *General Hospital* signaled the turn of the day: time to think about dinner. Since moving to Dandelion Drive, food had lost its pleasure. She had a large pot and a small one, a frying pan, a spatula, and a wooden spoon. The stove's only working burner was a lopsided black spiral that heated on just one side. To sustain them, Robin made pasta and hot dogs and hamburgers fried in a pan. She bought deli meat and bread, rotisserie chickens, frozen pizza.

While Haley did her homework, Robin rummaged for two cans of soup, found creamy chicken with wild rice. She truly hated these soups, could taste little in them but salt and metal. The chew of the rice, the soft chicken, the creamy soup turning gelatinous the moment it began to cool. She put one can back in the cupboard, checked for bread. Toast, at least for tonight, was all she'd be able to stomach.

The smell of the soup, such as it was, had started filling the kitchen when there was a loud knock at the door.

Haley lifted her head.

"I'll get it," Robin said, but Haley trailed behind her. On the stoop was Cindy, a large paper bag in her arms.

"What are you doing here?"

"Brought you some halushki," Cindy announced as she walked past Robin, straight to the kitchen. Amber, who'd been behind Cindy, glanced at Haley and came in too.

"Never freezes as good as you want," Cindy called. "Made way too much today."

Robin joined her in the kitchen. The smell of the cabbage and bacon overpowered the soup, and Robin turned off the burner.

"Hope I didn't fuck up your dinner plans," Cindy said. She eyed the soup, a skin already forming on the thick white surface. "Guessing this'll be an improvement."

"Smells amazing," Robin said. She was so grateful, and suddenly so ravenous, that she thought she might cry.

"Yeah, well, thought I owed you, after last night."

"That wasn't your fault."

"Sort of was though, right?" Cindy pulled two beers from the paper bag and opened them. "Let's eat."

Robin took four plates from the cupboard and sat at the table with Cindy and the girls. Cindy served each of them a pile of steaming halushki, butter and bacon grease spreading to the edge of the plate. Robin pressed her fork through the cabbage and noodles. On this raw winter night, after a day of expenses and defeat, it was the best food she'd ever had.

They ate in silence. Haley cleaned her plate but didn't look up once. When she asked if she could be excused, Robin nodded. Amber glanced at Cindy and followed Haley into the living room.

"Want any more?" Cindy asked. There was at least another serving in the dish.

Robin shook her head.

"I'll take it for lunch," Cindy said. "Need a break from the snack bar hot dogs."

Cindy put on her coat and packed up her casserole dish. "Amber, let's go."

The girls were sitting on the couch, tapping on their phones. Cindy assessed the room while Amber zipped her coat, her eyes running over the water stain on the ceiling, the crumbling plaster, the boarded window.

"This place is a dump," she said. "Thought a slumlord would live in a fucking palace."

"Traded the palace for your apartment's new linoleum and countertops," Robin said. "And windowpanes."

Cindy raised her chin. "Clyde'll do the install," she said. "Called this morning, begging like I knew he would. Least there's that."

"Thanks," Robin said.

Cindy opened the door for Amber. "See you around," she said.

"See you," Robin said.

Cold air rushed in through the door when they left. Until that moment, the house had been warm. It was quiet now, but the kitchen still smelled of bacon and cabbage, and there seemed a bit more light, a bit more air.

CHAPTER 10

Every day the *Four Points Bulletin* was delivered to Dandelion Drive, the leftover subscription of a previous tenant. Robin stacked the issues by the kitchen garbage can, uninterested in the basketball scores and school band photos that passed for news in Four Points. On Monday, however, the front page, all-caps headline caught her eye: "WHY NOT HERE?" Below was a full-page drawing of an impeccably restored Cassatta Building in downtown Four Points. Each window on all four stories was bordered with ornate stonework. The entryway was a lantern-lighted vestibule with a stained glass mosaic overhead. It was stately, with the solidness and authority its hundred-year existence may very well have deserved. *The goal of Coketown Investments: from eyesore to event space,* the caption read.

Robin stood the paper upright. The rendering, carefully drawn and detailed, was a break from the usual articles about spaghetti dinners and incidents of child neglect. More than different: it was hopeful.

The article, which began at the bottom of the front page and continued to page three, detailed Coketown Investments' plan for the building to be an affordable community event space with apartments on the third and fourth floors. A representative from Coketown said, "No one puts any faith in small towns, as if the good stuff belongs somewhere else. We don't buy that. Why not here?"

Why not here? The newspaper took up the challenge. Over the next four days, *Bulletin* reporters featured the most egregiously blighted properties in Four Points to highlight how radical a project Coketown was undertaking.

First, front page: *Four Points' Blighted Downtown.* Underneath a large picture of the old community center was a caption: *The Four Points Community Center, once a vibrant cultural meeting place, has been vacant since being purchased by Tom Frost in 1996.* There were other pictures too: the crumbling foundation, numerous broken windows, a blurry image of a rat in the overgrown weeds out front.

Asked for comment, Tom Frost offered none.

The next day, the reporter focused on the Professional Building overlooking the river. *The Professional Building has been unused and unmaintained since being purchased by Daniel Hilson in 1997,* read the caption. *In 2000, a falling brick damaged a parked car, and in 2002, the pigeon population required city intervention.*

The Prospect Building, city-owned, was the next day's subject, specifically the city's failing, years-long struggle to secure the budget for demolition. Mayor Videllia took the opportunity to announce the building's sale to Coketown Investments.

"We're pleased beyond words," said Mayor Videllia. "Coketown will be announcing restoration plans in the months ahead. This is an exciting day for Four Points."

Throughout the days' worth of articles, photographs of dour Four Points streets littered the pages. Robin's houses weren't among them, but they could have been. Each moldering exterior looked more or less the same.

The final subject of the series was the burned-out shell of the Riverside Hotel and the Way Car, site of the Landlord Association meetings. Five years prior, a ceiling collapsed and injured a kindergartner living with his family—illegally—in a third-floor room. The debris pinned the child's leg, causing paralysis. The article named Tom Frost, again, as the owner.

The series concluded with a short reaction from Coketown Investments. "There are obvious problems here," they said. "We hope this is the beginning of great change in Four Points. We want the best for the people of this community.".

Great change. Change was the last thing anyone expected—or wanted. Robin couldn't understand why, of all there was to work for, someone had chosen this.

*   *   *

The Landlord Association met a few days later. When Robin arrived at the Way Car, Tom stood, grim, with the newspaper tucked under his arm. Before he had a chance to speak, a woman wearing a lavender coat and a metallic purple scarf swooped in, showily waving a stack of papers.

"Autographs, please," she shouted. "Tom Frost—the great slumlord of Four Points!"

Tom clenched his jaw. "The city should be thanking me for keeping these places off their balance sheet," he said. "I'm doing them a favor."

The woman sat beside Robin. Her hair was thick and dark, fanned back from the sides of her face in a way that emphasized the crows' feet at her eyes, the veins of plum lipstick bleeding from the edges of her lips.

"Micheline Royer," she said, putting a hand on Robin's. "So sorry for your loss, honey."

"For Chrissake, Micheline," Tom said. "You'll be as screwed as the rest of us if Coketown starts a big push for residential property improvement. Let's not fool ourselves—that's the next step."

"A lot of people are pretty excited about what Coketown's doing."

"Really, Micheline? Are they? Are *you*? Don't answer that."

"I *am* excited. This is good for Four Points, good for pretty much every single person in town except yinzes. Or did you forget? I take care of my properties. You try to find one person says they have issues with my management."

"They got issues with your gallery," Danny Hilson called out.

"Who does?"

"Just sayin' what I heard."

"My gallery's the best thing happening downtown. That and the Cassatta—we're going places." She rustled in her enormous handbag. "I want you to read this." She slid a piece of paper to the middle of the table. "You're so scared of Coketown, their money, their plans. Time to make some plans of your own. This is a grant," she said. "Pittsburgh Region Landmark Preservation Grant. Mostly meant for local governments, but there's nothing that says one of us couldn't apply. 'Honor the structure and add cultural value to the surrounding area,' it says. Could keep outsiders away. If that's what yinzes want, let's do it."

The men responded with derisive snorts.

"A *grant*? What are we? A bunch of fucking do-gooders?" said Hilson.

"Let's get a grant and add solar panels to our properties," said Ryan Snyder. He was laughing so hard he could barely get the words out. "Let's add fancy compost bins. Organic gardens."

Micheline shrugged and took back her paper. "You're a bunch of ignorant pricks," she said. "Laugh all you want as other developers come in and put their own million-dollar skin in the game. Pittsburgh's tech market is growing, fracking's gonna be huge—there'll be newcomers. They'll want nice places to live, and they'll have money to pay for them. But keep your dumps, if that's what you want."

"Alright, Micheline," Tom said. "You've said your piece."

"You haven't heard the half of it," Micheline said. She leaned over the table, close to Tom's face. "You miss being married to me," she said. "Am I right, guys? He misses me."

Tom cut the men's laughter with a hard stare, then regrouped. "Let's move on," he said. "Let's talk about who wasn't called out by the damn *Bulletin*—Coketown Investments."

The men murmured.

"We all know they've bought some pretty rough spaces," Tom said, "but I'm the one getting slammed in the goddamn newspaper for a duplex that needs a little paint. They get nothing for the Cassatta, which is basically condemned."

"Didn't they submit that plan to the paper?" Robin said. "Looked pretty nice to me."

"Right now it's a drawing," Tom said. "The building's same as it's always been—a disaster."

"People trust them," Micheline said.

"That's what I don't get." Tom rubbed his hands together. "They're outsiders. Come in with money from who knows where, and they can do no wrong. I don't get it, and I don't like it."

"They're gonna start thinking they can get away with stuff," added Ryan Snyder. "Who're they accountable to? Who's watching them? The group of us here—hell, we're good, law-abiding citizens, and we got the whole town on our backs. What about them? They as upright as they say? Someone should give them the same kind of message."

Tom Frost raised a hand to stop the buzzing anger. "One more thing," he said. "Don't think for a second they're not aiming to go residential. Take a look." He drew an envelope from a folder. "Got this in the mail, from Coketown. An offer for my place out on Whistlestop Road."

Robin took a sip of beer to hide her shock.

The men clamored for the envelope, but Tom held it out of reach. "Offered me $120K," he said. The men grew suddenly silent. "Now that's a hell of a lot of money, even for a big house like that. And you know what I said? I said no. Wrote back with that on a sheet of paper—*no*. Because if they start fixing up houses, that's the end for us, understand? They come to you, you do the same. It's a reckoning."

Robin was more surprised than she should have been that Tom owned that house. Someone had to. But to actually know the owner as well as she knew Tom brought the house too close. She could ask to go inside—and she didn't want that to be possible. Like running into men from her past at Walmart: too much proof that now and then were woven together, interlaced.

The meeting broke up with the men tense and quiet. Micheline nudged Robin gently with her shoulder as they walked outside.

"Hey," she said, "this is good for us. Coketown's got the men in a froth—perfect. No one's had the balls to help this town before. You and me, we can make a difference around here too. Screw these guys. Bunch of greedy bastards."

In another life, maybe, Robin could side with Micheline, but this was not that life. Circumstances required her to share the landlords' determination to squeeze as much profit as possible from their properties without the distractions of upgrades and maintenance. That was her only way out.

She didn't want to explain this to Micheline. Instead she said, "That house of Tom's—on Whistlestop Road. Does he have a tenant?"

"Please," Micheline said. "That place is a health hazard. Haven't been in myself, but Tom bought it a few years ago and basically deadbolted the door and turned his back. Doesn't want to renovate and can't rent it out. Figures he'll tear down the house, do something with the lot. He'll never get that far. Bet you know the place— way up on the hill. Overlooks the river. Might fall in there one of these days."

Robin fought to keep her voice steady as she hurried to safer ground. "You're opening an art gallery? Here?"

"Sure am," Micheline said. "Bought myself the old drugstore on Ember couple of months ago. I've got local artists, and I'll host lots of events. Don't say it," she said with a wry smile. "Not the most logical choice for Four Points. Come see me tomorrow. You'll be surprised."

Robin was too rattled to do anything but agree.

It was a relief to be in the quiet car, alone. Before going back to Dandelion Drive, she drove to the Cassatta. Her stomach lurched as her car rumbled over the uneven pavement on Main Street.

The landscape—raw, hilly, the river on her left and mountains against the horizon—was the only one she'd ever known. Money and education made Mount Rynda different, but beyond the nice homes was a world identical to this. It was all coal country, or used to be, and it wasn't always terrible. Long before she was born, businessmen made millions here, gaining wealth from the coke ovens in the foothills. Now the crumbling mansions scrolling past Robin's window—turreted and bay-windowed, original stained glass black-clouded but intact here and there—were barely audible echoes of the town's better years. Most had been split into rentals long ago.

When she reached the Cassatta, she pulled to the curb on the opposite side of the street. The Cassatta Building and its parking lot covered half a block. Four stories of crumbling red brick, every window missing or broken, weeds reaching from the openings. The large picture windows at ground level were gone, covered with graffiti-tagged plywood. Stonework surrounded each window, most crumbling or missing but some complete enough to suggest the building's former grandeur. A century ago, this red brick giant would have attracted Four Points' wealthiest coke families. Now, the roofline was uneven, with bricks and stone flourishes half-gone. The sidewalk in front of the building was cordoned off with blue police barriers and yellow hazard tape. The Cassatta was actively falling apart, in a state well beyond the CONDEMNED sign on the door.

Robin eased away from the curb, satisfied that her instincts had been right. The Cassatta was a mess, without any potential whatsoever. Coketown—whoever they were—were fools, and maybe Micheline was too. At the very least, Micheline was a dreamer. Robin couldn't afford to lose herself to fairytale plans. Trying to turn Four Points around was a doomed effort. Robin almost regretted she wouldn't be here long enough to be proven right.

*   *   *

Micheline was waiting outside the gallery when Robin arrived the next day. With the clouded sky, salt-stained roads, and empty storefronts, Four Points may have been the most desolate place on Earth. Surely no place could be as hollow, as brittle. Robin tucked her chin into her collar as she approached Micheline, whose bright lavender jacket was the only glint of color on the street.

"Are you ready?" Micheline called out, her voice yanked into the wind. Robin kept her chin down and raised one gloved hand.

When Micheline shut the door against the cold, Robin's ears thrummed with the gusts outside. For one long, frozen moment, she focused only on the sudden warmth against her face, the golden light, the absence of wind.

"You made it," Micheline said. "You're here." She unzipped Robin's coat for her, slid it from her shoulders. "Voila," she said. "My gallery. Follow me."

Robin moved beyond the threshold, drifting into a celestial netherworld. Micheline had attacked the space with her own wild vision. The walls and ceiling were thickly painted in midnight blue, absorbing the light from the street. Large, wide swirls of silver glitter swooshed across the walls as though propelled by their own energy. Heavy, sculptural metalworks hovered from the ceiling on bulky chains.

"Micheline, I had no idea," Robin said.

"No one does." She climbed the ladder, a bucket of spackle hanging from her arm. "I designed it on my own, and I'm doing it on my own. Well, much as I can. Had somebody in here to fix some wiring, and this is how they leave my walls." She indicated telltale mars on the swirls of midnight blue. She slicked on a bit of spackle with a wide knife, her motion confident, and when she pulled away, the repair was smooth enough to be barely visible, except for its color.

"It's amazing," Robin said. "Really."

"You're the only person I've invited here," Micheline said. "You're the only one to get a sneak peek."

"None of the landlords?"

"No way. It's killing them, not knowing what I'm doing over here. They think I'm crazy," she said mildly, "so I let them go on thinking it. But they'll see." She gave Robin a small smile. "You think I'm crazy too?"

"It just seems like so much work. For what?"

Micheline shrugged as though the *why* of it was hardly a consideration.

"We have a lot in common, you and me," she said. "I think we can help each other. I know what it's like, being forced into this. Got started that way myself."

"What way?"

"Necessity. A girl's got to live, right? And I'm too old to wait tables. Can't take the men anymore. Jackasses thinking they can say what they want. No thanks. I did my time. So what'm I supposed to do: Work at Walmart? Work the checkout at the Shop 'n Save? Can you see me there, really?"

"It's a paycheck," Robin said, thinking of Cindy. "Some people don't have a choice."

"Well, I decided to choose something different. I had a little money saved, and I went in with Tom Frost on a little place out on Hickory."

"You and Tom?"

"We were neighbors as kids. Married for too long. A real jerk when he wants to be, but it's served him well. Anyway, I bought him out a year after we got divorced and got my mobile park on my own."

"So you made it work."

"Oh, I've had some close calls. Deadbeats, busted pipes, lawsuits. I'm okay, mostly. I have a little extra. Or I did, until I decided to open my gallery." She pulled a stepladder to the opposite wall. "Enough of this. Let's go see the art."

She led Robin to her office at the back of the gallery, cluttered with boxes and large paper bags.

"It just started coming in," she said, pulling a few thick envelopes from her desk. "I put a little ad in the *Bulletin*.

Nothing flashy, but word got out that I was looking. These came this morning. Gary Butke's the artist. He runs Swickly Auto and started doing rubbings of the shattered windshields he got in the shop. He said they reminded him of exploding stars. Isn't that poetic? They're framed, so all I have to do is hang them." She opened the flaps of a large cardboard box, brimming with driveway gravel. "This is a collection of rocks that apparently show the face of Jesus," she said. "Helen Carver's been finding them for years. She said there's sixty-one rocks in here, and she wants every one of them back."

"Micheline, this is—"

"Crazy. Totally. But will you look at these? Definitely faces. Right here is a cheekbone. I think I'll set these out on a table." She reached for a poster tube. "This one's a little more traditional," she said, unrolling a long strip of paper. "It's a watercolor of a sycamore outside Connie Scant's kitchen window. She told me she has no idea why she painted it. She'd never painted anything before. She went out and got some Crayola watercolors at Walmart and started working on this last year."

"Micheline, it's hideous."

"Is it? Look at the way the trunk splits into the three branches—you can tell she really worked to get that right. I get why she wanted to paint it. It's a beautiful tree. Been here longer than any of us."

"You're really going to display these?"

"Are you kidding? I couldn't ask for better." Micheline showed Robin a poster from Margaret Brycelyn, who ran the Hometown Smile: a collage of handwritten order slips dating back fifteen years.

"She liked the handwriting," Micheline said. "She said so many different girls come through that place, waiting tables for all kinds of reasons, and they just leave these little bits behind."

Even though Robin left Four Points well before any of these girls would have poured her coffee, she felt she knew them already from their fat rounded g's, their i's dotted with tick-size circles.

There was too much to take in. Five paintings a man named Dean Smith had done of his dead cat, Riddle, with blood-caked fur and a crushed back leg. Ten black-and-white photographs of trains approaching and departing the Amtrak station on Water Street. A glass bottle of water and sand from the Youghiogheny River with a tiny plastic boat floating inside. A halfway decent oil painting of pink-blooming dogwoods outside the library.

It was so strange—people *wanted* this. They wanted art and a place to see it.

"I should go," Robin said.

"Okay," Micheline said. "Sure, you should go. But Robin—think about what I'm saying. We don't have to buy into what those guys believe. We can do something else."

Robin knew she should admire Micheline for her vision. Instead, she felt pity. Robin had lived her entire adult life covering ugliness with gilded smiles, relentless poise. She'd excelled at it—but it didn't work here. Some things would always stay in darkness.

Robin was sorry to leave the gallery and return to the cold. The wind woke her from the drowsy calm that had settled over her. She was back on Earth again, on the dirty streets of Four Points, far from the glittering galaxy of Micheline's wild, misplaced hope.

CHAPTER 11

Mid-February. Haley was at school. Robin was glancing at her mistakenly delivered *Bulletin*. She sipped her coffee, grimaced. She hadn't heated the water long enough, and the instant grounds floated in her mug. She dumped the weak coffee in the sink. Rage, always simmering, flared. Somehow, East Green was to blame for this, for everything. The apartment was a line in red, a constant drain on her resources.

She'd asked Tom Frost to help her make a punchlist, and today they were meeting at the apartment. Tom was implacable as usual. He turned on the water in the kitchen and bathroom, flushed the toilet, tested every outlet with a three-wire receptacle tester from his heavy black box. He opened and shut the windows. He heated each burner of the stove. He confirmed the temperature of the freezer, checked for bugs and mouse droppings in the drawers. He measured the space, pressed his palms against the exposed lathe beneath the crushed plaster, jiggled the metal framing overhead.

"Way you talked, I expected severed heads in the closet," Tom said. "What you've got here is a whole lot of ugly. You're right about that. No way to rent it as is." He knocked on the countertop. "Good news is, your punchlist don't got any of the big boys."

"Big boys?"

"Electric, plumbing, heating. Place ain't pretty, but stuff works. Once you clean up, it'll be livable."

"You're kidding."

"Understand your situation. You need a tenant."

"Soon."

"End of March, I figure. You do a few things. I mean that: a few. You wanted my advice, here it is." He pulled a pencil and the familiar spiral notebook from his bag. "Your punchlist, in order of importance: clean it out. That's first. Your squatter was a pig, but most are. Next: rip up the carpet and linoleum and put in new linoleum for the entire space save the bedroom. Leave that carpeted and rent a steam cleaner. You can do your own lino, easy. Ceiling tiles are a quick fix—get replacements for the broken ones and push them in. Get some guys to plaster the holes in the wall and paint over it. You wanna get fancy, you can add some outlet covers and change out the overhead bulbs to 100-watts. That's it. A good week's work, you'll be ready to list."

"What about the missing cabinet doors? And the fridge is so old."

Tom shook his head, held up his hand. "Would you live here? Would I? No. But someone will. It's safe, it's solid. I'm assuming the downstairs tenants won't cause any problems. Someone will be lucky to find it. List it at $450 to start. Next year, bump up your downstairs tenants to match."

"I don't know, Tom."

"Shame you have to do this much, honestly. Squatter should be held accountable. Makes you mad, right?" He tore the sheet of paper from the notebook. "Like I said, cheap lino, cheap ceiling tiles, plaster. Clean it up. Done." He eyed her. "You okay?"

Robin nodded. "It's a lot of work. Even doing what you said. If I can do this—"

"You will."

"—rent it and somehow figure out how to rent out Dandelion Drive, I'll almost have enough coming in to get a small place in Mount Rynda in a few months. Get back home." So much could derail this plan. Robin pushed those thoughts aside.

"Well, good luck," Tom said. "You listen to me and don't go overboard, you'll be alright. Ain't no time for Pottery Barn." He reached over, took the punchlist back from her, crossed out *paint plaster*. "Skip it," he said. "Save your money."

When Tom left, Robin considered the apartment, trying to imagine the *after* while facing this sordid *before*. She appreciated that Tom was trying to save her money, but sticking to his punchlist was ludicrous. Not replacing the missing cabinet doors? Maybe Tom and the other landlords didn't distinguish between frugal and negligent—maybe Ray hadn't either—but Robin did.

How could he have tolerated owning a place like East Green? Ray had been taking money for these properties for years. Maybe he had a grand vision, like Coketown. But Robin knew Four Points too well to really believe that. More and more, she feared that Ray was like every other landlord, aiming to do just enough to keep a property from collapsing.

None of this was unreasonable. She'd seen how destructive and unpredictable tenants could be. Still, in the back of her mind was a tiny whisper of protest. People around here didn't ask for much. And neither did she. She'd always gone along with what Ray wanted, content enough to keep her masquerade afloat. She knew she'd been an easy wife. Ray carefully cultivated their life in Mount Rynda, expecting Robin to follow suit. If she'd balked—if she'd thrown a wrench in the works like a broken water heater did in one of these properties—she wasn't sure what Ray would have done.

When Ray had considered what a Four Points tenant did and didn't deserve, he probably wasn't thinking about her—she'd done everything she could to bury that connection. But she *was* connected. This had been her home. Ray's negligence toward his tenants suggested a lack of respect she couldn't help taking personally, even as she counted the seconds until she could get out of town. Would it have killed him to put in a decent lock to keep a squatter out? Was fixing the damp-rotted ceiling at Dandelion Drive really so much trouble?

Robin heard a rapping and a man's voice saying, "Hello?"

Startled, Robin turned. Kevin Trundel raised his hands.

"Didn't mean to scare you," he said. "Was going to call, then heard you up here."

A girl stood behind him, blown-out hair, tapping on an iPhone with expensively manicured nails. Acrylic tips, airbrushed in red and black swirls, rhinestones on each pinky.

"What's up?" Robin said.

Kevin stared into the apartment. "Wow. Griffith made a freaking mess."

"You knew the squatter?"

"He came down one night to bum a smoke. Dude was intense." He looked around again, shook his head. "Listen, me and Damien need some new locks. Don't want to get into it, but there was a situation. I'll put 'em in, just need you to get 'em."

"Sure. No problem," Robin said. She had no idea if buying new locks was her responsibility, but she was glad he'd asked permission. "I'll get them to you tomorrow."

"Thanks," Kevin said. "Good luck. People do crazy shit, right?"

*   *   *

Robin headed to Home Depot, grateful for an errand. If she relaxed, made a cup of coffee and sat with a magazine, she risked feeling comfortable—as though her rundown, broken-windowed house were home. She couldn't bear that.

A salesman pointed her toward the locks in aisle twenty-three. She was deciding between deadbolt kits when she heard angry voices the next aisle over. She stopped, listened, ears pricked, a startled animal. The voices swelled, a man furious about a sold-out brand of snowmelt, a Home Depot employee wearily responding. Robin didn't care about the argument. She listened for cadence, timbre, tone. Because the voice— the man's voice—sounded like Vincent Latimer.

Shaking, she peered around the end of her aisle. There he was, Vincent, standing in front of an endcap display of snowmelt. He was flushed, overheated in his heavy woolen coat—paunchy and gray-haired, ever so slightly stooped, his cheeks sagging and loose. How old would he be—seventy-eight. An old man. His coat, clearly expensive, was salt-brushed like his dirty snow boots and crumpled jeans. He'd been here through the winter.

Robin slipped back out of sight, heart pounding, her palms sweating around the locks' plastic packaging. She waited. When Vincent left the aisle, she followed. He favored his right leg, leaning heavily on his oversized shopping cart, full of bags of sand and buckets of salt. Twenty years pressed down on her. Vincent Latimer in Four Points. A lifetime ago, when he was a much younger man—and Robin, seventeen—the only thing tying him to Four Points was the train line that delivered him once a week. Apparently, things were different now. The cart full of winter tools, the layers of salt on his boots, the boots themselves—he lived here.

"You have enough?" the employee asked, placating. "May not be able to get back for a few days."

"I'm not worried," Vincent said. "It'll snow, then it'll melt. That's it."

It'll snow, then it'll melt. The matter-of-factness of those words, the impatient, weary black-and-whiteness, was achingly familiar. When Vincent turned toward the checkout, Robin sat on the edge of a model tub. To steady herself, she focused on how the solidness of the porcelain pushed into the backs of her thighs. She put a hand on her deer charm, pressed its antlers into her skin.

He wasn't supposed to be here. His life was in D.C.

She'd gone with him once, a year into their affair. A secret overnight trip suggested by Vincent impulsively one night at the Gleason.

"I don't have a train ticket," she'd said.

"We'll buy one onboard. I'll take care of everything."

Robin had gotten a friend to cover her shift at the Rowdy Buck and listened as Vincent made the necessary calls: his wife, to tell her he wouldn't be back the next day as planned; the Regis Union Station, to book a room; Caspar's, to reserve a table for two at eight o'clock.

They overslept the next day and had to rush to make the train. "Go. Go. Make this light," Vincent said. "Park by the station. There—that one—right there."

"It says no overnight parking."

"Just park, damn it," Vincent said. He was already counting out bills. "I'll pay for any tickets."

Robin had queasily obeyed. She hurried after him in the teetering heels she'd worn the night before, falling into line behind two men with briefcases and navy wool suits. The train was already rumbling closer, closer, rushing past them, finding its precise position on the track.

Only when Vincent was handing his ticket to the conductor had he remembered Robin.

"Right," he said tightly. "I need to buy one more."

As the train heaved away from Four Points, the smooth, powerful sound of the rails guiding the train was unlike anything Robin had ever heard. She'd turned to Vincent, smiling, but he'd busied himself with papers from his bag.

Hour by hour, she'd kept her gaze on the view beyond the window. Every turn of the track uncovered something new, a copse of trees or a crook of river previously unseen. When the conductor announced their approach to Horseshoe Curve, declaring it a historic railroad engineering landmark, Robin pressed closer to the glass and could see the entire length of the train hugging the side of the Allegheny Mountains. They sped past a viewing platform from which a few people waved, saluting the passengers as they continued on their grand adventure. There were other towns in Pennsylvania besides Four Points—of course there were—but still somehow it surprised her to see train stations signposted with other towns' names and the well-dressed people coming on with their trim rolling luggage, heading for the city. When the train entered Maryland, it was the first time Robin had ever crossed a state line.

They pulled into Union Station at rush hour, emerging from the underground tracks into a bustling, suited-up crowd. Briefly, Vincent took Robin's elbow, just long enough to steer her into the flow.

"Stay with me," he said, hurrying past shops and bars and trench-coated couples embracing on escalator stairs.

Ahead was a drugstore.

"Wait," she said.

He turned, irritated. "What?"

"I need a toothbrush. Some makeup."

"Right." He took two twenties from his wallet. "I need to make some calls. Meet me by those phones."

What pained Robin most when she thought about this trip was how surprised she'd been by what happened and how much faith she'd had even at the moment when Vincent put the wrinkled bills into her hand.

"Something came up," Vincent said when she'd returned with her bag. "You go to the room, order dinner for yourself. I'll be over later."

"Order dinner?"

"Room service. They'll charge my card. Just—stay there, okay?"

He walked her to the hotel, checked in at the desk, went as far as the elevator before waving goodbye. Robin went to the room alone. She let herself in with the key, turned on the lights, set her purse and shopping bag on the king-size bed. The only hotel she'd ever been to was the Gleason, and that was only to visit Vincent. Robin told herself she was furious, that he was a hypocrite—he never thought she wasn't good enough when they were at the Gleason, and he asked her to do things he wouldn't dream of asking his wife. Robin tried to rile self-righteous rage. But when she pulled open the curtain and gazed at the traffic-choked street below, she began to cry.

She'd wanted to call Cindy but didn't know how to dial out of the room. Besides, she already knew what Cindy would say: that for men like Vincent, slumming it was a phase, a hobby to indulge in before going home to his wife. Robin's problem, Cindy never missed the chance to point out, was that she thought Vincent was different from every other guy who ever set foot in town looking to buy or sell a piece of Four Points when really he was just another asshole. Cindy was so crass, so *hard*, but she wasn't the one sobbing in a hotel room two hundred miles from home.

Robin didn't order room service. Instead, she went back to Union Station, ate a BLT and chips at a deli, and cringed when she handed over her carefully guarded bills.

Vincent was waiting in the room when she returned. "Where were you?" he demanded. "I told you to stay here."

"Vincent? Why are you so mad at me?"

Vincent closed his eyes. "This was a bad idea. Too risky. A guy from my office saw me come off the train—he asked me to have a drink, and I couldn't say no. Our wives are friends. If he tells her I'm here, I'm done for."

"So go home. Say you wanted to surprise her." Robin felt desperate to make him happy.

The look that shadowed Vincent's face had electrified every nerve in Robin's body.

"I should," he said tightly. "But I need this."

He grabbed Robin's arms and pulled her roughly to her feet. His neck had a sour, sweaty smell from the train ride. He hiked Robin's legs around his waist. He yanked her shirt roughly over her head. He pulled her skirt down as he undid his zipper with his other hand. He pushed himself into her, hard, thrusting and groaning so that the mattress shifted on its frame. Robin tried to slow him down—he needed to put on a condom—but when she pushed his shoulders back, he shook off her hands. She didn't insist. He wanted her. The more-familiar territory was a relief. Robin felt him throbbing, hot liquid pooling inside of her, leaking onto the bedspread. Vincent pulled free, not saying anything when he went into the bathroom. After a while, the shower went on. Robin, shaking, cleaned up as best she could with tissues from the box by the bed.

She couldn't get into her car, drive home, and fall asleep in her own bed. She had to wait for him to emerge, dripping, from the shower, his erection half hard. When he leaned over her again, kissing her breasts and lifting her onto him, she had nowhere to go but with him back into the shower, where she sucked him off as he shouted and pounded the tiled walls. He leaned deep into the water as he came, and Robin nearly choked as water rushed over her face, into her nose and mouth.

After, Vincent was kinder. He rubbed lotion into Robin's back and arms and helped wrap her in a hotel robe. He opened two beers from the minibar, one for each of them, and found a movie to watch on TV. In the morning, Vincent walked her to the train tracks, bought her a cup of coffee, and told her he'd see her in a couple of weeks. No kiss, no hug, nothing but a furtive glance around them as he returned to the escalator and disappeared.

He didn't return to Four Points for over a month. When he finally did, summoning her to the Gleason with a playful, dirty voice as though the D.C. weekend had never happened, Robin told him she was pregnant. He counted out five hundred dollars and said, *Just take care of it*. She never saw him again.

Wouldn't he be surprised to see her now, sitting on a Home Depot bathtub, his younger-man's mistake, to hear her say, *I kept the money and the baby too*? If that were the story, if that were her triumphant tale, if she could whip out her wallet and press a photograph of his handsome, beloved son into his face, she'd do it. She'd shove the picture down his throat until he choked.

That wasn't the story, of course. Trevor was dead, and Ray was dead, and Vincent—she wanted to put her hands around his throat, she wanted to bury a shovel in his head—was pushing a cart through Home Depot, alive.

CHAPTER 12

Cindy Sweeney was restocking juice in aisle five when Robin found her at Walmart. "Push that trolley over here," Cindy huffed. "Fucking juice bottles. Two-fucking-fifty for cran-grape. Shit."

Robin handed Cindy two bottles from an open box. She regretted coming here, initiating contact with Cindy, but she needed to talk to someone, and Cindy was the only person who knew enough to understand.

"You remember Vincent Latimer?" she said. "Trevor's father?"

Cindy kept lining up bottles, a neat column of ruby reds. She didn't respond.

"Cindy. I saw him today at Home Depot. He's in Four Points. He was shopping for snowmelt. I think he lives here."

"I know."

"You *know*?"

"Saw him in here about three months ago. Barely recognized him. Old fucker now, ain't he?"

"What the hell, Cindy? Why didn't you tell me?"

"So you could—what? Meet for some fucking beers? Your life is shitty enough, okay? I didn't want to pile on. I was being kind, get it? A friend."

"You're not a friend."

"Used to be. And that's the fucking point. It's over. The past is fucked. Let it go. Who cares if he's here or in fucking Siberia?"

"What's *wrong* with you?" Robin felt her restraint leaking. "You know what happened. He's not just some ex-boyfriend you ignore in the checkout lane."

Cindy was already shaking her head. She started lining up mango-oranges with unnecessary force. "Bad idea."

"You don't even know what I'm going to say."

"Hell I don't. Leave him be, Robin. It's been over a long time."

"Don't you think he should know what happened?"

"Hell no."

"You're wrong."

A scrawny woman with a cart shuffled into the aisle. She reached past Robin for a bottle of tropical fruit punch. Cindy adjusted a bottle of mango-orange so its label was perfectly parallel with the edge of the shelf.

"Here's what I think," she said when the woman was gone. She kicked the trolley toward a rack of beef jerky. "You been back, what, a month? Month and a half? You still don't get it: People are here, Robin. Living their lives, going about their fucking business. Everyone but you. Then you come back and act surprised. *Annoyed.* That's bullshit. You're gonna see people. Even people you wish you wouldn't. Hell, look at us, talking like old friends."

"This is different. It's *Vincent.*"

"Not different. I see people every fucking day. No one gives a fuck. It's Dave. It's Jerry. It's Wayne Jabborski. Remember him? Wayne? He beat me up once. Now I see him all the fucking time. Do you understand what I'm saying?"

"Forget it." Robin began walking out of the aisle. Beneath Robin's rage was a hurt that surprised her.

Cindy owed her nothing, and Robin expected nothing besides hassle and unpleasantness. Still, to not tell her about Vincent's existence in Four Points, even though Cindy was the only person in the world who knew what Vincent had been to her—this was a betrayal.

"Robin," Cindy called.

Robin did not turn back.

"When are you going to stop chasing him?"

Robin flinched. Struggled to keep walking away.

The town looked different as Robin headed back to Dandelion Drive. Darker, with shadows over the road. Another blizzard was coming, more snow pressing on the icy gray remains of the last storm. Robin drove slowly. She didn't trust herself on the Ember Street Bridge. The Yough below was liquid pewter, numbing, so cold it would feel hot against her skin, her scalp. She stared forward, leaned close to the wheel. She tried to believe that the road would not warp under her tires, that the river would not rise to meet her. She tried to focus on Haley, who'd be sitting on the living room floor with a bowl of ice cream, the wail of *General Hospital* starting up. The image shimmered, then faded.

*   *   *

Robin kept busy all morning, neck craned from the top of a stepladder as she scrubbed bleach into the yellowed water stains in the corner of her living room at Dandelion Drive. Some of the paint flaked off, leaving the whole corner damply pocked, so she sanded until she was certain there was an active leak under the eaves that would require more work than she could possibly manage or pay for. She should have left well enough alone. When she couldn't sand anymore, she lined the kitchen shelves with new floral shelf paper. It felt indulgent, standing sock-footed in her own home instead of addressing any one of the hundred income-affecting issues she tacked onto her to-do list daily. But Dandelion Drive was a rental too, or it would be one day. At some point she'd need to cover the sticky, mildewed surfaces. The busywork didn't much improve the place, but it tired her and filled the day.

The doorbell rang, threatening to introduce any number of problems. Robin laid the shelf paper aside. It was Cindy Sweeney, wearing a dark gray sweatshirt with a huge, open Rolling Stones mouth on the front.

"Got something for you," Cindy said, holding out a strip of curling receipt paper with a scrawled address: 3 Larkspur Road. "The old fucker pays for his adult diapers with a personal check." She pushed past Robin into the house.

Robin flinched. She should have been used to Cindy, but sometimes the barbed words angled just enough to slice her. She read the address again, not fully believing it was his. Vincent was in D.C.—instead of white marble monuments and cherry blossoms, Robin had always imagined Vincent's disapproving face, the back of his trench coat slipping from view.

"It's what you wanted, ain't it?" Cindy said.

"I can't believe he's really here. That he has a house."

"You wanna ride past?"

"Sometime, maybe."

Cindy scoffed. "Bullshit. Let's go. I'll drive."

"What if he sees us?"

"Fuck if he does?"

They went straight through town. Larkspur Road was about ten miles away from the business area of Four Points. Cindy turned at Sheetz onto Route 50, which took them out into pastureland and a few newly constructed homes. They passed the old glassworks, long, low, windowless. Closed since Robin was a teenager, it had once employed most people in Four Points at some point in their lives. The heavy black boots her father wore each day to the factory were on the stoop the day he left. For the rest of Robin's childhood, they used the plates and glasses he'd brought home, chipped or other-wise flawed, unfit for sale.

There weren't many houses out this far, just a few lights through the trees. Self-reliance was crucial here, as was a preference for solitude. When Robin knew Vincent, he'd been anything but isolated—his life was cluttered with too many parts and people. Now it was him and the bears and the rattlers. Him and the run-ning white-tailed deer.

The road was so curvy Robin felt a wave of motion sickness. She cracked her window and put her head back.

"You ain't pregnant, are you?"

Robin shook her head.

"Alright. Don't puke in my car."

It hadn't snowed in days, but the farmland scrolling past their windows was still pristine with hard-packed leftover snow. Cindy's heater blew hot air into Robin's eyes, and she angled the vent away from her. Robin expected Cindy to turn down the heat or apologize for Robin's discomfort, but instead she said, "This is some-thing, ain't it? Me chauffeuring you around after you ignored me for twenty years."

"I didn't ignore you."

"You didn't even tell me you were leaving. You ever wonder how I found out? I went to your old place—the Rowdy Buck—and when they told me you quit and went to Ike's, I went there. When *they* said you quit, I knew. Didn't get much information from those gals, but they said you met some rich guy during the dinner rush and moved to Mount Rynda. They thought it was the great-est thing, like you'd won some waitress lottery. And all I could think was, *Man, I could tell you some stories.*"

"I'm sorry I left without telling you," Robin said.

"I knew you so many fucking years," Cindy said. "I wondered about you, you know? Wondered what happened to you. What your life was like in fucking Mount Rynda. You ever miss us?"

"No."

"Fair enough. You ever think about us, at least?"

"There was no point. I never planned to come back." The car was so hot. She adjusted the vent again, then lowered the heat herself. The gusting air quieted. "But you stopped. You stopped what we were doing."

"You ain't the only one who can change her ways," Cindy said. "It was time for a new life, so I got one. Like you."

It was nothing like her. In no *way* like her. Every move Robin made since abandoning Four Points had been calculated to ensure that her life was nothing like Cindy Sweeney's. She was about to call her out, explain how wrong—absurdly wrong—she was, when Cindy slowed the car.

"Larkspur's just ahead," Cindy said.

They turned onto a narrow two-lane road lined with bare-branched, old-growth trees. After passing a small white bungalow with a porthole window above the front door, they didn't see another house for several minutes. Finally a large, dark red home came into view on the right. It had plain siding and a plain shingled roof. A brick chimney let out a thick cloud of cozy smoke, and a pretty glass lamp shone in a bowed downstairs window. Robin imagined Vincent inside, reading a newspaper by the fire.

Robin couldn't remember what had prompted her to go looking for Vincent on that day twenty years ago. Maybe work had been a little too hard, and she was tired and wanted her life to change. Mostly, she remembered feeling desperate to forgive him and desperate to show him she was worthy of another chance. He'd always made her so desperate. She'd left a sleeping Trevor at Whistlestop Road with Cindy and went to the railroad tracks to find him, certain he'd talk to her once he found out she'd had his baby. Trevor was nine months old, perfect, beautiful. Of course Vincent would want to know.

While she waited for him, a westbound CSX train rumbled by, the heaping yellow coal cars sparkling as the rocks' flat faces caught the light. The coal train went on. Its whistle was a low, half-hearted heaving of old breath.

Another train approached, a sleek passenger line as out of place in Four Points as a rocket ship. No one was waiting in the Amtrak shell, but a Honda sedan raced the train down Water Street. At the station, a man jumped out of the passenger side and waved briefly to the driver. Robin scrambled out of her car as the train came to a stop.

"Hey!" she yelled.

The man turned.

"Man named Vincent Latimer always takes this train— you seen him lately?"

"The guy with the mines?" the man called back, stepping into the train. "Hasn't been here in months."

That was it. That was how easy it was for him to leave her.

Life had always been different for Vincent than for Robin. He hadn't spent the last twenty years haunted by what happened that day after she came back from the train tracks. He could just leave everything behind, move on.

Except he hadn't. He'd come back. He was living in Four Points, on Larkspur Road.

"Pretty fucking nice," Cindy said, staring at the house.

Robin took another look. She could almost feel the warmth inside the house, see the shelves of books.

"I thought it'd be darker." Robin tried to laugh. "You know. Bones in the yard."

They drove past slowly, but the road was too empty, the area too desolate, to pull over unnoticed. Cindy K-turned a hundred yards beyond the house.

"So what do you want to do?" Cindy said.

They passed the house again. It shrank in the rear-view mirror.

"Knock on the door? Throw a stone through the window?"

"Don't be ridiculous."

"For fuck's sake. We drive out to the fucking *wilderness*, and that's it?"

"I just wanted to see where he lives. For now."

"So you do want to do something."

"No. I don't know, Cindy. What should I have done—strangle him with a garden hose when I saw him at Home Depot?"

"Now you're talking." Cindy turned onto Route 50 to take them home. "But let me ask you something. If you could pick one person to talk to, who would you choose: Vincent or Trevor?"

"What an awful question."

"Who would you pick?"

"Trevor. Obviously."

"You can't."

"I can't be obvious?"

"You can't choose him. He's dead."

"Don't talk to me about Trevor."

"Why not? You all talked out on him?" Cindy rolled down the window and lit a cigarette. "I bet you've never talked about him. You just went on with your brand new life and tried to pretend it never happened."

"You didn't even go to his funeral, Cindy! You were my only friend. Your mom went with me—remember that? You stayed home and drank a forty. Don't bother apologizing. I'm actually grateful. If I'd had someone to carry me that day, I might not have made it."

"Who are you fucking kidding? You still would have found yourself a Ray."

"I can't listen to this. Let me out of the car." Robin pushed on the door handle, not really meaning to open it, but the door suddenly swung wide. Robin grasped for the handle, bracing herself against the buffeting wind.

"Jesus Christ, Robin! Close the fucking door! Listen. I'm saying Vincent isn't Trevor. Telling him what happened isn't going to make anything different. Nothing'll change. Do you understand me?"

Robin could barely see through her pooling tears. "I'm so sorry you think I'm crazy," she said. "So sorry your landlord is a *maniac*."

"It's what I said before—about us living here with people from the past every single goddamn day. You know how we survive, Robin? How *I* survive, scanning their fucking Corn Flakes? I leave 'em be. I don't say nothing to them, they don't say nothing to me. Because what kind of hell would my life be if every fucking time I saw a guy, he wanted to stop and chit-chat? 'Hey, Cindy. Got two beef jerkies here and a gallon jug of ketchup. Still remember the hummer you gave me back in '88.' Jesus."

Robin laughed. Suddenly, harshly, the sound came out of her like glass shards in a blender. Was this happening? Every piece of her life converging and warping, a mish-mash of forgetting and forgotten, reanimated ghosts and laughter that shook her body. Then she and Cindy were laughing together, imagining checkout lanes and old mistakes, and Robin was hit with elation that was all shivers and shadows, no light. Half-crying, they made their way along the winding road that led, for now, away from Vincent.

*   *   *

After she tried to find Vincent on the train tracks that long-ago morning, she didn't go straight home. Or maybe she did. The time she was absent from that house seemed in retrospect to be endless, a lifetime with her son that she squandered.

Cindy was still in her pajamas when Robin got back to Whistlestop Road. "That was quick," she said.

Robin shrugged. "Heard he doesn't come out here anymore."

Cindy made a disgusted sound in her throat. "Prick."

"Trevor sleeping?"

"Yeah."

Robin wondered, in the years to come, if she'd felt anything unusual as she put her hand on the doorknob of Trevor's room that day. Some days, she was certain she had felt something—or *not* felt it—as soon as she'd walked through the door. The story she preferred to believe: right away, she'd known something was wrong.

In reality, she might not have suspected. She might not have known. She might have simply walked in and leaned over and lifted the baby and noticed that his lips were blue. His face was cold. His head flopped limply away from her arm. Robin righted his head and gave him a little shake.

"Wake up, sweets. Mama's back. Trevor. Time to wake up, sweets. Trevor."

Cindy appeared in the doorway. "He's really out," she said.

"Feel his nose," Robin commanded. "His hands. They're ice cold."

Cindy leaned over the baby, then straightened, her eyes wide, her face pale even under her thick foundation. "Jesus Christ, Robin. Something's wrong with him."

"Didn't you check on him? He's freezing. He should have had a blanket." She gave the baby another tiny shake. "Trevor? Open your eyes, Trevor. Trevor."

"I'm calling 911."

He was still, so very still. Robin was still too as she held her son and waited for help. The baby seemed to warm as Robin held him, the cold seeping from each tiny cheek to Robin's, the fingers releasing their iciness to Robin's palms. He just needed to warm up, drink some milk from a bottle. Robin put her nose against Trevor's wispy brown hair, so soft it barely felt human.

Once the ambulance arrived, it ended quickly. He'd died before Robin had gotten back. Any warmth she'd felt was her own skin pressing against cold, dead flesh. And it was funny, the way she screamed when they wouldn't let her take Trevor back to her room, where everything would surely return to normal, lesson learned: it was the scream of a devoted mother, a loving, responsible mother, not an aimless, self-destructive young girl.

Hardly anyone knew about Trevor. Cindy didn't go to the funeral—she was MIA when they left for the church—but Rochelle stayed with Robin the whole time. She didn't have anyone else to rely on. The waitresses from the Rowdy Buck came that morning too—a handful of permed middle-aged women in black, their makeup subdued for the occasion, their sensible waitressing shoes replaced with plain black pumps. They sat quietly through the service, listening to Father Ducio's exhortations to pray for this unbaptized child, locked out of heaven until prayers lifted his soul from purgatory.

Afterward, the waitresses gathered in a clump in the last pew to swap their heels for black rubber-soled flats and went to work. When everyone but Rochelle and Robin had left the church, Rochelle drove them home.

At Whistlestop Road, they found Cindy slurring-drunk, sitting on the porch steps with a cigarette and bare feet. Robin wanted to go inside and sleep for a thousand days.

Cindy stood, wobbling, blocking her path. "Thought about going to the church," she said. "Thought about praying. Fucking souls. Fucking hell. Fuck all yinz. Ain't my kid, you got that? Ain't my kid. This is you. It's on you. It's on you, bitch, you understand me? You let this happen under *my* roof. I took you in, gave you a room, and this is what you did, this is what you did to me—"

Robin slapped her. Cindy lost her balance, landed in the drift of snow on the porch. She put a hand to her cheek, numb and red from the cold, and laughed. Laughed and laughed and laughed. Robin went inside as Rochelle began yelling: *What the hell's the matter with you, it's freezing out here, pull yourself together, you hear me? Get inside, what the hell are you thinking—*

Once things quieted down, Rochelle came to Robin's room, knocked on the door, sat on the bed.

"She's having a rough time," Rochelle said. "Broke all our hearts, you know?"

Robin had been crying so much it hurt to blink. More tears came, and she didn't bother wiping them off her face. Rochelle put her arms around her, let her cry.

After a few minutes, Robin said, "I'll get over this, right? I'll move on?"

"Oh, honey," said Rochelle, stroking her hair. "You don't get to *move on* in Four Points. You'll get by, but you ain't moving on from anything long as you're here." Rochelle squeezed her. "I'll go get you a beer."

Robin's head throbbed. As she sat on her bed, her grief and guilt heavy as boulders around her neck, she knew she'd do anything to be free of them.

Twenty years later, the weight was still there. Hidden, buried, but just as heavy. Compressed like coal into a diamond, or like an ugly, invasive irritant layered and wrapped and worried into a pearl.

CHAPTER 13

They'd lose their house in Mount Rynda tomorrow.

The bank would take over the house and change the locks on February 21. Today was February 20, the last day to use their key, step inside. In the morning, Haley came into the kitchen crying, so Robin kept her home from school and decided they'd say goodbye. *To the house*, Robin clarified too many times. *Not to Mount Rynda. We'll be back in Mount Rynda by spring.* Her mantra. The words that kept her sane.

Before they left, she texted Steph for the first time in weeks. *I'll be at my house at noon. Bank takes the keys tomorrow. Stop by?*

Steph replied immediately, an emoji face mid-scream. *I'll be there.*

Mount Rynda drew closer mile by mile, the traffic sparse. Haley watched the road, her head resting against the window. A scene from every long trip in the car. Summer trips to the Outer Banks, late nights returning from Kennywood, Haley just barely awake in the back seat. Sleeping, she had so much in common with the infant Robin clutched tightly in her arms.

Haley, her second child.

After losing Trevor, Robin's life gained a single purpose: get out of Four Points. She moved out of Rochelle's house, found a room with a waitressing friend, took a better job at Ike's Tavern and worked herself to the bone so she'd sleep without dreams. She made decent money. Her memory was good, and regulars knew they could relax with her as their waitress. Their drinks would be methodically refilled. Their special requests would always find their way to the kitchen. Robin's eyebrows would never rise even if they sat at the same table with a different woman every night of the week. She would never get a booth of men laughing, but she wouldn't forget the ranch dressing they asked for with their fries, and the next time they came, the ranch would magically be there, creamy and cool, without their having to say a thing.

Ray became one of those regulars, requesting a booth in her station whenever he came to town, sourcing stained glass from a local factory for some of his high-end clients. He liked barbecue sauce instead of ketchup, and the steak in his sandwich cooked rare. He never had to tell her anything twice, and Robin, for her part, sensed a civility in him. A desire to keep things cordial, never exploring the dark corners of life.

She began to shed her old life, getting rid of her bright-colored Wet n Wild and letting the indigo-black fade from her hair. She cast off everything she'd done along with the tubes of plum lipstick, the stained plastic combs. In that way, nothing felt like a lie—she could grieve for Trevor and never let it impact the life she was reaching for. When Ray finally suggested she move with him to Mount Rynda, she left as easily as air being exhaled away.

When Robin became pregnant with Haley, she was certain it was only a matter of time before the truth came out—this wasn't her first pregnancy. Surely her doctor, tracking her belly's growth, would recognize a woman who'd done it before. He suspected nothing. The new pregnancy became the only pregnancy. She feigned nervousness and naiveté when other women shared stories of labor and birth. And, in private, she mourned. She'd gotten so used to the idea of hiding Trevor's death. Only as a pregnant woman did she realize she'd also been hiding his very existence. She felt she was killing him again, more permanently, more cruelly, than ever. This time, the killing was purposeful, selfish: revealing him would rob her of everything. With a snug new baby girl in her arms, she couldn't fathom risking that.

When Ray drove her and Haley home from the hospital, Robin sat protectively next to the car seat in back. He reached through the space between the front seats and touched her knee. He smiled in the rearview mirror.

"Almost home," he said. The words were as good as a padlock, sealing Robin's former life away forever. To Robin, what echoed in a grim whisper was, *Home free.*

As she drove to Mount Rynda now with Haley, she remembered what she had felt that long-ago day: happiness without contentment, relief without any promise of rest. What amazed her most was that shallow, frothy Mount Rynda had buried her secrets so deeply, so well.

Haley was gazing out her window, her face hidden from Robin, her thoughts unknowable.

"Home sweet home," Haley murmured when they finally pulled up to the house.

Robin nearly wept. The sidewalk was unshoveled, as were the steps to the porch. Robin let them in with the key she still had on her keyring—not the ring of heavy, jangling slumlord keys but her other one, her real-life one, with her car key and leather tag imprinted with the Coach logo. The door felt heavier than she remembered. Though the furniture was gone, the air smelled—strangely—of old cinnamon. As soon as she kicked off her boots and felt the cold wood under her socks, she needed to steady herself to keep from collapsing.

Haley pushed past her and went upstairs, to the empty room that had been hers.

Though there was no legal restriction on visiting, Robin felt irrationally conspicuous. Soon she'd be locked out of this house, but nothing prevented her from returning to Mount Rynda whenever she wanted— every week, every weekend, often enough to visit Kim for her regular manicures and to keep up, over lunch, with the teary, endless stories of Steph's impossible teenage son.

But there was everything stopping her. Absolutely everything.

There was no sound from upstairs. Haley may have fallen asleep on her bedroom floor. Robin gazed out the French doors in the kitchen onto the wet, snowy deck. Impulsively, she opened the doors and stepped outside, rubbing her arms in the freezing air. She shuddered—and not from the snow seeping under her socks. She and Ray had thrown their famous summer cocktail parties on this deck. Robin spent days planning and shopping and cooking the spread their friends and Ray's clients had come to expect: cheeses and olives, spinach and mushroom rolls, artichoke dip, guacamole, stuffed mushrooms, chicken satay, tomatoes and mozzarella, skewers of shrimp from the grill. Silver bins full of ice and bottles of wine, a table with liquor and mixers, Ray presiding behind the simple wooden bar by the kitchen door, shaking whatever signature cocktail they'd chosen that summer, painstakingly researched and rehearsed and always, always a success. Ray loved these parties, loved the annual tradition, and Robin went full-throatedly along.

She never told Ray how much she dreaded them. She didn't mind the shopping and cooking. What she dreaded, rather, was how afloat she felt amid the people. How exposed. Singly or in pairs, it was easy enough to be Robin Besher, Ray's wife, with her rainbow of merino cardigans, her closet full of ballet flats, her polite conversation. But in a crowd, she would get a feeling that was something akin to drowning.

Her life—a life she loved, a life she tended to jealously, clung to like a life preserver—would turn on her, push her under: The fifth holiday party of the season, each with its own little black dress, each with the clients and familiars who kissed her formally on the cheek then swept Ray to the bar, leaving her with the women nursing their wines. The expectant, assumptive call from the school, requesting a weekend's worth of volunteer work on the silent auction. The monthly Women's League luncheons, a revolving cast of tablemates, the endless capacity other women had for discussing their housekeepers and petulant German au pairs.

In crowds, nights with Vincent raced silkily through her mind. The memory always left her feeling calm and strong. *I was that girl, I did those things, none of you will ever know what it felt like with that man, in that bed.* The women Robin knew in Mount Rynda would never envy any part of Robin's past. Though Robin had gratefully left it behind, she sometimes relied on scattered bits as though they made her better than the soft, coiffed women pouring weak iced tea and trading horror stories about gut kitchen renos running ten grand over budget and fancy bathroom tiling (*And my designer said this was the best, the absolute best Italian tile you can buy*) that arrived in the wrong shade of beige.

She stepped back inside.

"Knock knock," a voice was saying from the living room. Robin turned: Steph, already blotting tears with a Kleenex. She strode quickly toward Robin and hugged her. "You disappeared on me," she said, but the accusation was mild. "God, this is terrible. I just can't believe it. Your *house*, Robin. You lost your house. Is Haley here?"

Robin nodded, closed her eyes, squeezed the bridge of her nose. "Upstairs. She's devastated. We both are."

"Tell me what you need. Anything."

"There's nothing you can do."

"I can't believe that. Why didn't you tell me you were out of money? I would have loaned you whatever you needed."

"I know. But the problems Ray left me are bigger than that."

They were quiet.

"Well then. I won't stand here and cry." Steph pulled a wine bag from her enormous gold leather tote. "This is for you. Drink it, smash it, whatever helps get you through this."

Robin peeked at the bottle—their favorite chardonnay.

"Call me. You never do. But call me. I'll be waiting."

She was gone. When Robin finally went upstairs, she found Haley sitting by the window, knees hugged to her chest. Haley jumped up and pushed past Robin to the stairs, unwilling to show her tears this time. And then, for the final time in her life, Robin locked the door.

While the engine warmed, they looked at the house. *Their* house, for one last moment. Warm air finally blew from the vents, and Robin put the car in gear.

Haley didn't turn from the window once as they drove back to Four Points. Her hand moved to her face. Robin heard her sniffling.

When Haley stopped crying, Robin said, "Will you talk to me? Tell me how school is?"

"It's fine."

"How about Amber? Is she leaving you alone?"

"It's fine. We're, like, friends now."

"Wait—you're *friends*?"

"We bike around. Whatever."

Robin kept her eyes on the road to hide her alarm. She hadn't realized Haley was biking anywhere after school, in the dead of winter, let alone biking around with Amber Sweeney. "Where do you ride?"

"I don't know. Around the neighborhood."

"What do you talk about?"

"Seriously?"

A question too far. Haley changed the subject quickly, believing, as children often do, that she was being subtle.

"You know that house?"

"Which one?" They knew so many houses now.

"The big one. At the top of the hill. Everyone knows it."

"On Whistlestop?" The words came out choked. "You mean the house on Whistlestop?"

"Yeah."

"What about it?"

"Was it always like that?" Haley asked. "When you were younger. When you lived in Four Points."

Robin held tight to the steering wheel. She was afraid, irrationally, of driving them over the median and into oncoming traffic. Since moving to Four Points, they'd scarcely spoken of the fact that Robin had lived there as a child. Robin had actively avoided the subject.

"No," Robin said. "It was different, I suppose. It's been neglected for a long time."

The answer seemed to satisfy Haley since she turned back to the window. Why she wanted to know, Robin couldn't say. And she was terrified to ask.

They arrived in Four Points just before school let out. The roads were sleepy and gray. One street was closed for construction, so they had to wind their way through downtown, past the Cassatta.

The exterior had been changing daily: scaffolding in new places, netting wrapped around upper floors, industrial chutes appearing from top-floor windows, aimed at dumpsters below. Workers moved around, masks over their faces, amid the buzz and shriek of power tools. The ground around the building was piled with large pieces of debris, and the building had a lightness—so much dust and damp torn away from the great bones of the structure, like a shedding of excess fat or heavy layers of unwashed clothes. Or— Robin tried not to think of it this way—a casting-off of something weighty and tangled that made it difficult to breathe.

A few men with hard hats were huddled over a large blueprint, fluttering in the cold wind. Where the dumpster had been was a flatbed with tall stacks of bound two-by-fours—Robin knew enough to recognize that the interior framing was beginning. She watched the workmen, discussing the plans intently. One of them, clearly the man in charge, stepped onto the street, put a hand to his hat, peered at the roof. Square jaw, gray bags above his cheekbones. She gasped—it was Vincent Latimer.

"You know that guy?" Haley asked.

"No," Robin said quickly. She didn't know how she managed to keep her voice calm. "A long time ago, maybe. He looks familiar."

They drove past Vincent and the other men. The car windows were tinted. There was no way Vincent could see inside. Robin made herself remember that. She made herself drive calmly, slowly, to the end of the block.

"Who does he look like?" Haley craned her head back, trying to get a look.

Robin made a turn, forcing Vincent out of their sight.

"No one you'd know," she said, turning the radio up.

CHAPTER 14

He was too close. Haley had actually laid eyes on him. She might remember his face, think about him—that was a bridge too far.

Haley went to the Sweeneys' for dinner. Under different circumstances, this would have worried Robin, but now she had business to attend to. And she knew she could trust Cindy with certain things, certain secrets. In a way, she'd been trusting her for twenty years.

Still, when she dropped Haley off, she didn't go up to say hello. She just flashed the headlights to Cindy's silhouette in the doorway and drove away.

It was pitch black at this hour, but she barely watched the road. She could navigate these streets in her sleep. Nearing Vincent's house, she pulled to the side of the road when she saw a car in the driveway. She felt perfectly calm. She'd known she needed to do this since she heard his voice in Home Depot, raising Cain over sold-out salt.

She would ask Vincent to leave. In her mind, it made all the sense in the world. He owed it to her. He'd ruined her life once. He could do it again—he had too much power—unless she stopped him.

She knocked on his door, her glove muffling the sound. Bitter wind brought bright tears to her eyes.

She took her glove off and knocked again. Vincent answered.

"Yes?" he said.

She couldn't speak. A newspaper in his hand, reading glasses on his head.

Finally, she said, "Do you know who I am?"

"Please, I'm very busy. I'm not interested in anything you're selling."

It happened so quickly.

"I'm one of the landlords," Robin said.

"Ah yes, the landlords," Vincent narrowed his eyes. "I've received a few letters from your kind. I suppose this is your doing then." He reached over to the side table by the door, grabbing something that Robin recognized as an envelope from a one-hour photo service. Inside were a few photographs, clearly of the narrow yard in front of the Cassatta. Recent, by the snow. A deer carcass lay sprawled over the lawn, pooling liquid coloring the ground pink.

The landlords. Of course, some had been angry enough to take action. It didn't take much. Those men were born angry. Just the look of the deer made her queasy. She gave the photos back to Vincent, careful not to touch him.

"No," Vincent said after reading her expression. "I don't suppose it was you."

The photos were clearly meant as documentation. For legal action, surely. Vincent may have been older, his hands gnarled by arthritis, but he was still dangerous.

They could destroy each other, for all she cared. But she didn't have that kind of time.

"Vincent," Robin said. There was no use putting it off any longer. "It's Robin."

Nothing. No reaction to the sound of her name.

She drew the deer necklace from beneath her scarf. "Robin Nowak. You gave this to me."

There was no flicker of nostalgia, no awestruck acknowledgment of the years. Only cold and sudden recognition, which Robin detected in the hardening of his face.

"What do you want?" he said. A hard wind gusted, rattling Vincent's folded newspaper.

"I need to talk to you."

Inside, her ears rang from the sudden absence of cold and wind. The house smelled like vanilla, sweet and chemical, and in the dim, drawn-curtained room she saw a candle burning on the mantle, ivory-colored wax in a glass bowl. On the wall was a dried berry wreath wrapped with gingham ribbon. The furniture was quaintly carved wood with plaid upholstery. She could have been inside a Cracker Barrel.

Vincent stayed close to the door, a hand on the doorknob. His hard expression had shifted, slightly, to unease.

"What are you doing here?" she asked.

"I live here."

"Since when?"

"A year now."

"Why?"

Vincent didn't move away from the door. "I'm doing what no one else will. Spending money no one else has."

"Pick a different town—anywhere in the world."

He studied her. Then he said quietly, "I always wondered what happened to you."

The fury came fast, overwhelming. "You don't have any idea what happened. The landlords?" She inhaled deeply. She shouldn't have told him anything, shouldn't have let him glimpse any aspect of her life. "That doesn't matter. That has nothing to do with what I have to say to you."

"Wait." Vincent moved away from the door. Next to where the photos had been was a soft, brown leather wallet. Vincent extracted a few bills. "Take it," he said, extending the money. His hand trembled. "I understand it's not what you came for. Whatever you want to tell me, I don't want to hear it."

"How dare you?" Robin pushed the money away, forcefully. "You owe me more than that, after what you did—"

She'd lost the thread. She struggled to breathe, to steady her voice, but it came out shrill. "Just leave us alone," she said, and she fled. She fumbled the car key into the ignition and pealed away, heart pounding, tears flooding. Whatever she'd come to his home to do would never be done.

*   *   *

The money wouldn't disappear.

It followed Robin in the days after her encounter with Vincent, hovering directly in her line of vision, ghostly, disconnected from Vincent's hand. It mocked her because she'd once taken money in just this way, and she was as desperate for money now as she was back then. *Take it*, the money whispered. *What's the harm?* Again and again, Robin swatted it away, but it shimmered back into her mind. He didn't know how far she'd come. She wanted so much more. She wanted to get back home.

The only thing stopping her was the nightmare of East Green. There was simply no way to accept that this was their life—and that one apartment, one terrible, squalid apartment, trapped them here. She would get her daughter home where she belonged. With Haley at school, the entire day ahead, Robin was going to bring East Green to its knees.

She was doomed to fail from the moment she opened the door. She had no paint cans, no laptop with instructional videos saved offline. She hadn't arranged for a dumpster. She didn't even have a crumpled handful of trash bags. Instead, she had Ray's tool box and, under her arm, a metal crowbar she'd scavenged from the dank basement of Dandelion Drive. She didn't pause to consider what she could realistically accomplish. Her shame was so acute, so hot behind her eyes, she could almost believe she could use it as a weapon—incinerating anything standing between her and freedom.

In the kitchen, the crooked, sporadic cabinet doors beckoned her. With her crowbar, she pried off each one, twisting the hinges, splitting the cheap particle board. She left them on the floor. She turned to the shelves and counters, littered with soup cans and fast food wrappers. A drawer held a few plastic dishes and cups with faded logos. Robin swept everything into a pile.

The open bedroom door exposed the stained beige carpet beyond, thin, with no pad to add extra bulk. With enough firm pressure, her box cutter blade sliced easily through. She tore long, jagged strips with a satisfying rip. They curled in unwieldy folds around her feet. She cut until her fingers gave out, shaking, her grip weak around the blade.

Winded, she sat on the gritty, bare subfloor. She forced herself to take a few slow, deep breaths. Snow clouds had darkened the afternoon, and she hadn't bothered to turn on a light. She did now—the stark bulb on the bedroom ceiling—revealing what she'd done. The apartment had passed a point of no return. She considered, briefly, burning it to the ground.

Her cell rang: Cindy Sweeney.

"What the fuck happened?" Cindy was at home, killing time before the night shift. "I know you drove out to Vincent's. Don't try to lie because I spotted your car when I was filling up at Sheetz. Unless you got some other business down 50, which you don't."

The tears came fast, unexpected. "I'm in trouble," Robin said, her voice cracking.

"What the fuck?"

"I'm at my place on East Green. I made a big mistake here, Cindy, made everything worse—"

"I'm coming over," Cindy cut in. "Don't fucking kill yourself before I get there."

Ten minutes later there were footsteps, and Cindy appeared at the apartment door.

"Holy hell," she said in greeting. "What the *fuck* did you do here?"

Robin put her head on her knees. "I'm never getting out of here," she said. "Everything I promised Haley was a lie."

"Get the fuck up," Cindy said. "What the hell is wrong with you? Get up. Get up, up, up."

Robin stood, brushed off her jeans.

"Better," Cindy said. She walked around the apartment and finally stood in the kitchen, by the pile of cabinet doors. "Start here. Let's sand one each. One by one. Piece by piece. All it takes. Okay? Jesus, I should be a motivational fucking speaker."

They sat together on the floor, sanding the chipping paint on two cabinet doors. It was physical work. Mindless, calming. When the sandpaper scraped her knuckles, Robin welcomed the raw flint of pain.

"So," Cindy said. "Your visit to Vincent. Tell me."

Robin, calmer now, told her everything. She told her about the money.

"Such a fucker," Cindy said, and she magically dissolved the specter of the bills in Vincent's wallet.

"I didn't tell him about Trevor," she said. "He didn't give me a chance."

"You'd be crazy to tell him."

"Why? He was his son. I can't keep that secret."

"Bullshit. He deserves nothing from you."

"No, he doesn't *deserve* it. That's not what I'm getting at. I'm saying it's fair, it's decent, to tell him. I'm a fair and decent person. Not telling him feels like lying."

"So lie. Who cares? You never told Ray the whole truth about your past."

"That's different. All of that was separate from Ray."

"You were a whore, and you lost a baby, and—oh, right, you blamed yourself for that—and you're saying this is *separate* from Ray? Your savior?"

"That was my own messed-up past. None of it made any difference in my life with Ray."

Cindy rocked back on her heels, her thighs winging to either side of her. "You've lied to yourself for so long you don't even know it anymore. You really believe you can put a lid on parts of your life like pieces of fucking Tupperware. Fine. Do that. We sell that shit at Walmart—I'll bring you some. But do it with Vincent too. He doesn't need to know about Trevor."

"I think you're wrong."

"Why?"

"Trevor was his son."

Cindy set aside the cupboard door and sandpaper. "Why can't you just say it?"

"Say what?"

"That you loved him. Vincent. I'm sick of you talking in fucking circles."

Robin was very still. Sanded dust drifted around her feet.

"He broke my heart," she managed to say. "He changed everything."

"So you owe him the truth for your grand fucking love affair."

"No," Robin said.

"You want his pity."

"No!" Anger flared. "Haley's waiting. I need to get home."

"Yep," Cindy said. "Me too."

Robin stayed back until she knew Cindy's car was gone. What a mistake, having her come here. Robin hadn't known she needed a friend so badly. Haley would already be home from school. There'd be homework to oversee, whatever reality trash Robin could find on the rabbit-eared TV, the last of the wine she couldn't afford. In the morning some version of this would begin again. Spring was way in the distance, as was Robin's promise to be back in Mount Rynda by the time the crocus buds peeked through. That dream had tilted over the horizon and dropped off the Earth—an Earth that must surely be flat because in no world she knew would she have wound up here. She was exhausted, a deep yearning beneath the weariness. She hurried down the steps, her mind focused on Dandelion Drive. She imagined again the evening ahead, eating bread and soup with Haley at the table, sitting on the couch to watch TV. They'd be warm, together, safe inside their makeshift home. It felt like life—a life in Four Points.

That was supposed to be impossible.

CHAPTER 15

The house was dark when Robin got home. No light on the porch, no light in the windows. Haley should have been home five hours ago. Robin had texted to tell her she was on her way back. Haley had texted back a thumbs up. There were no signs of forced entry, struggle, violence. The house was simply—empty.

Moments before Robin was planning to call the police, her cell rang.

She snatched up the phone. "Haley? Are you okay? Where are you?"

Haley was crying. She was trying to talk, but the words were blurred.

"Slow down. Haley. Tell me where you are, and I'll come get you."

"I'm fine," Haley finally choked out. "I'm babysitting. Me and Amber. Dana's not back, even though she said she was just going to the mall for a little while, and the baby won't stop crying—"

"Who's Dana? What baby? *Where are you*?"

Haley exhaled loudly, familiar teenage annoyance. "Amber met this girl Dana," she said. "She's a mom, and she's living in that awful house. We've been trying to help her, watching the baby, but she's gone, Mom. And the baby's screaming."

Robin's gut twisted tightly. Her daughter in danger. A *baby* in danger. Crying. Crying was okay. Crying was good. She forced herself to speak calmly, though what she wanted to do was shriek.

"I'm coming to help. You're not in trouble. I need you to tell me where you are."

Through the phone, she heard Haley say to Amber, "My mom's coming. What's this street again?" Then, to Robin, "We're at the house on Whistlestop Road."

*　　　*　　　*

"Tell me again what she fucking said."

"Cindy—"

"Don't 'Cindy' me. No way. Tell me." Cindy, in a Walmart polo, drew a small comb from her enormous purple handbag and began working on the tangled end of her long side braid.

They were on Route 129, a few miles from Walmart, heading back into Four Points. Robin clicked on the turn signal, pushing away her irritation. She'd explained already, after she'd driven to Walmart and had Cindy paged.

"The girls are at Whistlestop Road. They were babysitting for someone, a girl named Dana, who's apparently squatting there. Haley said they've been trying to help."

"Sounds generous," Cindy said, still combing out the end of her braid.

"They're in over their heads. The girl is gone, and our daughters are hysterical."

"Shit. Shit shit shit." Cindy pulled a cigarette from her bag and rolled down her window.

Robin knew better than to ask her to put it out.

"Did you have any idea Amber was mixed up in this?"

"I work for a living. Don't have time to keep my eye on her every minute."

"I'm not saying you should have known. I was just asking."

"Yeah, well, you should've been home tonight instead of trashing your piece of shit apartment. That's what *I'm* saying."

Cindy was right. Robin had lost track of Haley over all these weeks, relying too much on her daughter's independence and maturity. She was thirteen. Robin had left her alone after school nearly every day, chasing crisis after crisis, never stopping to consider there might be a crisis right under her own roof.

"Cindy."

"Yeah?"

"Does Amber know? About what we did?"

"You must really fucking hate me, asking me that."

"Will you ever tell her?"

Cindy inhaled smoke, held it in her mouth, let it out in a loud gust. "Got plenty of life lessons to teach without digging that deep. Jesus." She tossed the butt out the window. "Turn two blocks after the light," she said suddenly.

"What? Why?"

"Bet I know where this girl is."

"Shouldn't we get to Haley and Amber?"

"We will. This first."

Robin slowed at the light. They waited. It didn't change.

"Fuck."

"You think this is my fault," Robin said.

"Never said that."

"I don't know any more than you do. I have no idea who this girl is, or why she'd be at that house, or anything about a baby—"

"It's green. Fucking go."

Two blocks brought Robin to the entrance of the Laurel Estates trailer park. "Turn here," Cindy said.

"Cindy—"

"We'll find her, alright?"

Robin had spent periods of her childhood in Laurel Estates, bouncing in and out, trailer to trailer, as her mother got evicted and then scrounged up the cash for another month somewhere else. But that was all a long time ago, and Jolene was fifteen years dead.

Robin drove along the rows of trailers. Cold air washed in from Cindy's open window. Music was blasting from trailer #24. Cars were lined up outside.

"Here we go," Cindy said.

Robin parked five trailers down. Even from there they could hear shouting.

"Come on," Cindy said. She knocked hard on the door. Knocked again.

"Who is it?" a voice called.

Cindy said, "Looking for Dana."

A blond guy in a Coors t-shirt opened the door, not even trying to hide the joint in his hand.

"Is Dana here?"

He closed the door in her face.

Cindy pounded again on the door. This time, a girl answered—red-eyed, loose-jawed, the smell of whiskey drifting thickly across the threshold.

"What?" she said. The blond guy appeared again at her side. She leaned into him, barely able to stand on her own.

"You Dana?"

"Nope. Kendra."

There was a crash inside, angry shouting. The blond guy disappeared. Kendra pushed past Robin and Cindy and vomited beside the stoop. Then she collapsed on the icy ground. Another girl—tall, with stringy brown hair—emerged from the trailer and crouched beside her.

"Turn her over, goddammit, don't let her choke." Cindy hunkered down to help the girl turn Kendra onto her side. "Go get a glass of water and some paper towels, her hair's right in the puddle."

The girl ran in and returned a minute later, handing the water and towels to Cindy. The girl and Robin watched as Cindy lifted Kendra's head, wiped her mouth, and offered the plastic cup. After a moment, Kendra rose gingerly to her feet and went into the trailer without looking back.

"Thanks," the girl said to Cindy.

"Bunch of idiots," Cindy said. "We're looking for Dana. She here?"

The girl paled so quickly that Robin knew immediately it was her. "You CPS?"

Cindy said, "No. But our daughters are watching your kid, and if you don't get back there, I'll call them myself. Come on, let's go."

"My coat," Dana said. She disappeared into the trailer, then came out in a tan trench that Robin recognized.

"We've met," she said, surprised. "I saw you on the Ember Street Bridge. I gave you a ride."

Dana nodded, and they got into Robin's car.

"Now, who the hell are you?" Cindy said.

"Dana."

"Yeah. Dana what?"

"Katusic."

"I don't know any Katusics."

"Most of my family's out by Shelk."

"Who's your baby's father?"

"You can't ask her that," Robin cut in.

Cindy rolled her eyes. "The baby has a father, doesn't she? She? He?"

"She," Dana said. "Emma."

"Pretty name."

"Thanks. The father's Mark Ott."

"Ott—a John Ott lived near me at Hemlock Court a few years ago."

"That's his dad. We went out there a couple times."

"Kind of a lazy ass, wasn't he?"

"Mark's the same," Dana said. "I didn't even tell him I got pregnant."

Cindy looked meaningfully at Robin. "Maybe you got some sense after all."

They drove the rest of the way to Whistlestop Road in silence. Robin pulled to the curb. Though lights glowed in the cracks between the boarded windows, the house looked as forgotten as ever. The CONDEMNED sign fluttered on the door.

"It's fifteen degrees outside," Cindy said. "Can't have a baby in an unheated house."

"There's heat."

"How?"

Dana shrugged. "Just comes on."

"The owner keeps the heat on for a squatter?"

"I guess."

"Who is it?"

"Don't know. Some old guy."

Dana had to be confused. Tom Frost owned this house. By providing heat and light, he was essentially renting to Dana for free. It was generous, benevolent—and foolish. Heating a house with so many broken windows was like heating the backyard. Robin couldn't imagine Tom Frost agreeing to that in a million years.

"How long have you been here?"

"Couple months." Then she said, "Thanks for the ride," and opened the car door.

Cindy moved to get out of the car.

"Wait," Robin said. "I can't go in there."

"Like hell you can't."

Robin tried to steel herself. Her daughter was inside. She had no choice but to follow Dana and Cindy across the yard and onto the porch.

When Dana put her hand on the knob, Robin said, loudly, "No!" She heard the sound of the word, felt the quick slide of the *n* at the back of her teeth—but the command came from outside of her, from some person or point beyond what she knew.

"Cindy, this is insane."

"The girls are inside," Cindy said. "Open the door, Dana."

The key glinted in Dana's palm.

"I don't want to go in there," Robin pleaded. It was already too late. Had been too late since the moment Haley called her.

Inside, Dana walked quickly up the stairs, her coat and shoes in a pile on the floor, rushing to get away. Robin remembered what she was to a girl like Dana: an emissary from an adult world that intended nothing but harm. She knew this girl because she'd *been* this girl. Unapologetic, self-protective, wary. In the end, no one had harmed Robin but herself. She wanted to grab Dana by the arms and shake her. Tell her that the best place to direct her fear and distrust was inward.

Robin took a breath, nearly gagged.

The acrid stench was something physical, close and all around her. Too late, Robin covered her mouth and nose.

Cindy announced, "Piss. The piss of a hundred fucking cats."

"*Cats?*"

"The smell's in the walls."

Haley and Amber hurried out from the kitchen.

"Mom," Haley cried, running into Robin's arms.

Cindy stood apart from Amber. "You better explain what the *hell* you're doing here."

Amber glanced at Haley. "We found out someone was squatting here," Amber said. "We watched her sometimes through the window. We felt bad. We wanted to help."

"And you thought you could do—what? Amber. Look at me."

"Help her, okay? Bring her stuff. Watch Emma. That's the baby."

"Haley?" Robin said. "Is this true?"

Haley kept her eyes on the floor. There were tears on her cheeks. Not so long ago, Haley would have cried these tears into Robin's shoulder, leaving matted, wet blotches on her cashmere.

"Haley, answer me."

"The couch is full of mouse shit," Haley finally blurted out. "Someone is, like, threatening her. And—" Haley started crying so hard she couldn't speak.

"And? And what, Haley?"

"We were just trying to help her. We didn't know what to do."

"Who's threatening her?" Robin asked.

"Some lady said she'd call CDD. CFH. Something like that."

Cindy said, "CPS—Child Protective Services. They can take her kid if she gives 'em enough reason."

"Jesus," Robin said. "Poor girl."

There was no sound from upstairs.

"We need to go," Robin said. "Get your coats."

The girls disappeared into the kitchen.

Every second Haley spent here felt like a risk. Robin breathed through her mouth and looked around. Aside from the vile stench, the house wasn't much different from Robin's properties: filthy wall-to-wall carpet, chipped paint, dropped ceilings warped and stained, streaks of old paint at the edges of the remaining window glass. Worse, whoever lived here last had left behind a lot of junk. Empty pizza boxes and beer cans. Broken furniture, splintered window blinds, ratty curtains. Above the kitchen sink, a faded plaid half-curtain framed the river view.

There was the sense that at some point, long ago, long before Robin and Cindy did what they did within these walls, this was someone's beloved, lifelong home. Beyond the grime and garbage were shadows of what Vincent valued—the reasons for the high-priced offer Coketown had made to Tom Frost. The house was over a hundred years old, with architectural flourishes the wealthiest citizens of Four Points had once expected: ornate, wrought-iron grillwork covering the radiators; carved wooden baseboards and crown molding, thick with chipped layers of paint; glimpses of parquet where the wall-to-wall carpet was coming loose at the corners. Robin had never noticed any of it the years she'd lived here with Cindy. Now, with property on the brain, she saw it as an outsider would—as Vincent had. These details, however, did not endear the house to Robin. She found it all grotesque.

This was the house Robin had left that winter morning so long ago, her baby asleep. She hadn't even leaned into the pack-and-play to kiss him or to feel his steady breath against her neck. His bedroom was upstairs, but Robin felt the shadow of her son strongly where she stood. An ache rose in her chest, painful and hot. Robin had been waiting for a man who'd never wanted either of them, and her son had died.

"It hasn't changed," Cindy murmured. She jutted her chin toward the kitchen. "Even the fucking shelf paper is the same."

"Your mom had that little TV by the sink."

"All fucking day she stood in there, but all she cooked was shit from boxes."

"And canned chicken with gravy and toast. I remember that."

"At the end she lived on cereal and white bread with butter," Cindy said. "Shit."

From the kitchen, they could hear Haley and Amber talking in urgent, low tones.

"I can't believe Haley's been coming here," Robin said. "I can't believe I didn't know."

"Maybe it's different in Mount Rynda—helicopter bullshit and all that. I barely see Amber at home. She does her thing, I do mine. I buy the food, make sure she's got clothes and a home. Can't know everything she's doing."

"That's insane. I know everything about Haley. We're a team."

Cindy gave an ugly laugh. "Yeah? Haley's babysitting a squatter's kid in this godforsaken place. You had no fucking clue."

"It was a misunderstanding."

"Sure. Alright."

"She would have told me."

"You keep telling yourself that."

"I will because it's true."

Cindy pulled a few strands from her braid, wrapped them tightly around her index finger, and yanked them from her scalp. "Let's get the fuck out of here," she said.

They rode home all together, silence in the car.

CHAPTER 16

March 1. Rent collection day. Robin waited at home, anxious, pacing. Deirdre arrived first, on her way to the Shop 'n Save. The Trundels next, Damien waiting in the idling truck while Kevin ran the money up. Cindy had slid hers under the screen door sometime during the night, on her way home from Walmart. Nothing from Sister Eileen except an apologetic voicemail.

Better than last month. Not close to enough.

*　　*　　*

Dana and the baby were constantly on her mind. In Mount Rynda, Robin would have made a casserole. She would have baked a pie, or cookies, or banana walnut bread. She would have delivered the food in freezable storage containers that wouldn't have to be returned. New babies, new houses, hospital stays, deaths—on these occasions, Robin was usually the first of the women she knew to present her supportive offering. She wouldn't have dreamed of skipping a contribution or buying a pre-made item from Whole Foods. The particular expense of the ingredients, the time to prepare and cook them, the mess left behind in the kitchen—these were the sacrifices that gave the gift meaning. Without them, it was only food.

Even in Four Points, Robin couldn't shake the old compulsion. She went to Walmart and bought what she could: a box of diapers, a package of wipes, a loaf of bread, a jar of peanut butter, a bunch of bananas. Even a small bag of supplies was more than she could afford. She chose Cindy's checkout lane, grateful the store was quiet. She wanted to talk without being overheard.

Cindy rang up her purchases without meeting Robin's eye. She didn't say a word about the diapers.

Finally, Robin said, "I got some stuff for Dana."

Cindy sighed heavily. "This is a huge fucking mistake."

"How can you say that? She needs help. You saw her."

"Saw a train wreck, is what I saw. Not getting anywhere near it. Call CPS if you're so concerned."

"Why don't you?"

Cindy said nothing.

"Come with me later. Whenever you're done. I'll pick you up."

Cindy yanked her money drawer out of the register and slammed her fist on a switch that sent her aisle light into frantic flashes.

"I'm off at five," she said. "Be at my place a quarter after."

Cindy had her own Walmart bag when she climbed into Robin's car later that day, a gallon of milk and two boxes of Cheerios visible through the plastic. They drove to Whistlestop Road in silence, and Robin let Cindy lead the way to the front door. She knocked. Knocked again. Finally, Dana, in bare feet, boxers, and a t-shirt, opened the door. She had the baby on her hip.

"We're back," Cindy said easily. "You wanna let us in?"

"I don't need anything from you," Dana said.

"You got a reason to be scared of us?" Cindy said.

Dana stepped aside.

Robin held her arms out for Emma, but Dana turned so she was out of Robin's reach. For a moment, they looked at one another. Wordlessly, Dana walked across the living room to a folded towel on the floor. She lay Emma down, mewling, and unsnapped the white sleeper to clean and change her. The sleeper had been soiled, and Dana worked the squalling baby's arms and legs into a new one from a pile on the floor.

"We brought you some things," Robin said. "Diapers. Some food."

Dana sat on the floor with Emma, calming a little more than a wrinkled flour sack in the well of her legs.

"Haley said you're in some trouble."

"I guess."

"Can I hear about it?" Robin said.

"People getting in my business because I'm poor."

"Or because you're young."

Dana shrugged. "They assume I don't take care of my baby. They want to take her away."

"Have they said this to you directly?"

"Lady next door keeps telling me she'll call CPS. I don't even know what could happen if she does. I just want to be left alone."

"You have parents?"

"They kicked me out."

"Have you tried talking to them?"

"I was glad to go."

"It's hard being alone. You need help. Maybe that's what your neighbor is trying to do for you."

"Emma's *mine*," Dana said. "She's not a mistake I should have to pay for."

Robin took a deep breath. Dana needed more, much more, than Robin was able to give. She couldn't even make a hot meal to deliver in a foil pan. She should call CPS herself, try to get her some stability, some assistance. But the baby was cooing in Dana's lap. The house was so warm that Dana was barefoot. On the coffee table was a box of nut-and-fruit bars, a bottle of water. If only it weren't this house, this terrible house—

"You can call me anytime," Robin said. She took a pen from her purse, wrote her number on the back of a receipt. "Don't hesitate. Call for any reason. I want to help."

"Thanks," Dana said. She didn't reach for the phone number, so Robin placed it on the coffee table next to the bags they'd brought.

"Alright," Cindy said. "Let's go."

A few snowflakes blew inside when Cindy opened the door.

"Is this some kind of joke?" Robin said once the house was out of sight. "That house, that girl?"

"Girls like that all over Four Points."

"But that house."

"Houses like that too."

"You know what I mean, Cindy. Don't pretend you don't."

"This is bullshit," Cindy snapped. "This is total, complete bullshit. You think you can help that girl? She's fine. She's resourceful. Look at her—landed a place to live for free. What's she need from you?" She scoffed. "Oh, wait, I forgot. You're the civilized one, from *Mount Rynda*."

"That's ridiculous."

"You're right. What she really needs from you is money. And you're as broke as the rest of us."

"Her neighbors are threatening to call CPS. She needs some guidance, access to resources, someone to help her get some stability. You saw her—she's a kid. She's barely taking care of herself, let alone a baby."

"Think you can do better?" Cindy said. "Raise her in a slum rental instead of a squat?"

"If something happens to the baby, and we could have done something to stop it, we have blood on our hands."

"Don't seem to me like that baby's in trouble. Dana seems alright."

"She's young," Robin said. "You as well as anyone know what can happen."

"What can happen, Robin? An accident? A tragedy? Life's fucking chaos. Haley could get hit by a fucking drunk driver when she crosses the street."

"If someone had helped me with Trevor, he'd still be alive."

"Bullshit. Someone else could've put him in a four-teen-carat crib, and he'd have just stopped breathing. Because that's what happened, Robin—he just stopped. You know what I'm saying? Dana's young, poor, what-ever. She's a mom. She'll learn. She don't need you to teach her a bunch of bullshit about organic foods and fuck-all else. That's it. Trevor—fuck." She pressed her hands against her eyes. "Maybe you're right. Maybe we'll both go to hell. Who the fuck knows?"

"Don't you feel bad about what that baby's missing?" The words were out of her mouth before she could think. "Haley had so many opportunities in Mount Rynda. We had a beautiful home. She never wanted for anything."

"I don't fucking understand you. Ray lied the whole time about how much money you had, and you're still thinking he was this great provider."

"He was. He did provide. He didn't have to have the rentals. He wanted to start saving for Haley's college. He was good to us, Cindy."

"You kill me sometimes. I think you really believe the crazy fucking things you say. I think you believe Haley's better than Amber because she had a lying ass dad who happened to have money and bought you a house in a fancy city."

"Not *better*. I didn't say *better*. And I'm not talking about Amber—I'm talking about that baby."

"Let me tell you something." Cindy's voice was quiet. "Amber's dad was a drunk piece of shit. He stuck around for a few years, but anything we had was because of me. Always been that way. We don't have a lot, me and Amber, but we're okay. She's smarter than I ever was. I talk to her teachers, I make sure the homework gets done. And I hope she gets the hell away from Four Points one day. It's on her. She knows that. What's Haley learning from you? What've you got that someone else didn't give you? That a *man* didn't give you? Your great provider died, and the only choice you had was to come right back here."

Robin was shaking. "Get out of the car," she said. They were at a stop sign a few blocks from Nettle.

"You don't even have a fucking response?"

"Get out of my car. I don't have to listen to this."

"Fine with me." Cindy shoved open the door. "Count me out with your caretaking shit. I don't want no part of it."

Robin pulled away as the car door slammed. She felt sorry for Cindy, she really did. What did she know about marital support, true partnership? She'd had Amber's no-good father, then Clyde. Who knew how many men in between. Cindy had no room to judge personal choices, parenting choices, any choices. For the rest of the day, Robin tried to squeeze her rage into a tidy bundle of pity. All day, she failed.

*   *   *

Cindy was wrong. Dana may have acted like she didn't want or need Robin's help, but a young mom with a baby, alone in that house—nothing good could come from it. Robin understood that too well.

The next morning while Haley was at school, Robin retreated to her bedroom. The room was gloomy, sunless at the back of the house. She turned on a bed-side lamp, whose dim glow barely illuminated more than a sickly yellow sphere on the box she was using as a nightstand. She looked at the closet, resisted, then knelt and unearthed a box that was sealed with thick brown tape. The bottom was black-scuffed and shiny from decades of sliding out of the way; the turned-up edges of the tape were sticky with disintegrating glue. The box was the right size for Christmas decorations or off-season clothes, far too large for the ephemeral flatness of the memories it held.

She'd brought the box from Mount Rynda along with much more necessary things. She hadn't even thought about it—just made room among their boxes. The tape came up easily, releasing a dusty residue. She put the tangled nest of tape aside and opened the flaps. Even after so much time, the faint smells brought him back.

There hadn't been a baby shower. Robin's tips barely covered formula and babysitting. She bought clothes at Catholic Charities whenever Trevor's tiny feet began straining in his sleepers. Nine months of clothes, a few small toys—all he had, all he ever would have. Robin had kept every piece.

She hadn't done the laundry after Trevor died, had never washed his little clothes again. The basket had been full of soiled onesies and drool-stiff sleepers the morning she left him, and they stayed in that basket after, weeks turning to months. She knew she'd never recover if she gathered Trevor's laundry, so she pressed thoughts of it from her mind: his tiny clothes lurching in soapy water, spinning in the dryer, waiting for her to fold, fairy-sized sleeves fitted one over the other, limp footies matched and tucked against the chest that once shielded his live, beating heart. Eventually the dirty clothes went into a box with the rest. Her life as Trevor's mother reduced and contained and pushed aside to make way for everything that came next.

Trevor had died before he could do much more than hold and shake, and the soft toys jingled. There was a wooden rattle painted with bright stripes, a bear-shaped bell with a molded grip, a few plastic balls with loose bits inside—tiny spheres, a spinning disk, metal stars. A set of soft blocks with rubber loops meant for shaking and gumming. Three small rabbits, blue, yellow, white, with floppy ears and long, dangling arms and legs. Robin had tucked the rabbits at the foot of Trevor's portable crib, so large and empty for such a little baby. He didn't seem to have any idea they were there, but one night, late, when Robin peeked in on her way to the bathroom, one of the rabbits was tucked under his tiny arm, its long ears against his cheek.

Robin used a sleeper to push the rabbits into a corner of the box. She feared how they would feel against her skin.

This was it: dirty clothes and chewed-up toys. She hated the young woman who'd failed this baby in so many ways, hated that no one had told her she was doing everything wrong. If a woman like Robin had come to her, offering help, would she have accepted it? Been grateful? She hoped so. She hoped she would have seen the way forward and said, *please*—please save me from what could happen under my young, incapable watch.

Robin unfolded the baby clothes piece by piece. Even with a hot wash in strong detergent, these onesies and sleepers weren't fit for passing along. They were stained and stretched and pilled, secondhand to begin with, not the soft, velvety cottons that would promise a life drastically different from what Emma had known so far. A hand-me-down onesie, an old rattle—nothing here would signal Robin's intentions.

They couldn't stand in for what Robin had to do.

At the Shop 'n Save, she bought good winter foods—hearty canned soups, a loaf of whole-grain bread, apples, pears, a box of green tea bags, a brick of sharp cheddar cheese. Walmart would have been cheaper, but she couldn't risk a run-in with Cindy.

Alone, she drove to Whistlestop Road. When she parked at the curb, the neighbor's Dobermans gave their threatening welcome, lunging against the tarp-covered fence. She walked quickly to the porch. To her surprise, Dana opened the door before she could knock.

"Emma's sleeping," Dana said. "Come in, if you want."

Robin closed the door behind her. Dana didn't invite her to sit, so she held out the grocery bag.

"Some things to help keep you warm," she said. "Must get cold in here, even with the heat on."

"Not so bad," Dana said. "The broken windows have boards over them." She took the bag. "What are you doing here?"

Robin didn't move. "It must be hard," she said. "Having a baby so young, on your own."

"What do you know about it?"

"A lot, actually. I had a baby when I was nineteen. A little older than you but still pretty young."

Dana looked at her with more interest. "The dad stick around?"

"He didn't even know." Not exactly the truth but close enough. She held her breath, waiting for questions, but Dana didn't probe. Maybe she hadn't fully understood what Robin was trying to say. Maybe she thought the child Robin was talking about was Haley.

"You here to give me advice? Teen mom advice?"

"Not really." Robin half-wanted to scare her but knew that wasn't wise. "I want to help. Stop by now and then, bring a little food over. Okay?"

Dana nodded. "Alright."

Upstairs, Emma wailed.

"See ya," Dana said.

Outside, a maroon sedan was behind hers at the curb. Robin kept walking, watching as the driver leaned over to the passenger seat, lifted a plastic bag into his lap, opened the door.

Vincent Latimer stepped out.

It was impossible to avoid her. Vincent paused before slamming the door shut. The noise set off the Dobermans again. Robin stayed where she was, on the unshoveled, trampled walkway.

Vincent spoke first as he slowly approached. "Robin," he said.

"What the *hell* are you doing here?"

"This is my property."

"*Your* property?"

"Yes."

"Tom Frost owns this house."

"He sold it to me."

Robin knew immediately that it was true. Tom, like any of them, had a price.

The vacant house that had heat and light, the boxes of diapers, the fridge full of food—Tom would have forced the squatter out, not tried to help her. The benevolent "old guy" letting Dana live in peace—of course he was Vincent. Still playing the benefactor while shaping the world to please him. Still preying on a young girl with nothing.

"It's mine," Vincent said. "The house. Not the girl."

"You're disgusting."

"What exactly do you think is going on?"

"You haven't changed, have you? Head of gray hair, and you're as much a wolf as ever. That girl has *nothing*. She's just like I was but with much bigger problems. She's sixteen, Vincent. I could call the cops—"

"You've got this wrong."

"I should have seen it."

"Will you listen? I bought this property when I first moved here. I offered a good price. I got busy with some other acquisitions and didn't make it back over here for months. When I did, I found Dana."

"How convenient."

"I haven't touched this girl."

"I don't believe you."

"You should be careful what you say—you're trespassing on private property. *My* property."

"You have no idea what happened here," Robin said.

Before she could say anything more, someone yelled, at them or the dogs—Robin couldn't tell which—to shut up. A woman with a wool coat over her shoulders had emerged from the house next door and was swatting a newspaper at the Dobermans beyond the blue tarp fence.

When she spotted Robin and Vincent, she called, "Need to talk to yinz," then minced across the snowy yard in pink rubber-soled slippers. "Wait right there," she called again, and Robin did as she asked. Behind her, Vincent waited too.

The woman huffed closer. "You related to that girl?" she asked, jutting her chin toward the house.

"Why do you ask?" Robin said.

"Don't like what's going on," the woman said. "She got a baby in that dump. Hear crying day and night. I'm calling CPS, is what I'm doing."

"You don't need to do that," Vincent said smoothly.

"Hell I don't."

"We're supporting her. We're making sure the baby is cared for. You've seen me here, haven't you? I bring food. I make sure the house is warm."

The woman eyed Vincent, then turned to Robin. "First time I seen you," she said.

"Robin's a friend," Vincent said. "With two of us checking in, you don't have to worry. Here." Vincent took out a business card. "This is my property. You have any concerns, call me first, day or night."

The woman slipped the card into her sleeve, pressed her lips together. Behind her, the Dobermans were whining and pacing. "I'm watching that girl," she said. "Understand me? These kids, their drugs, their drinking. Don't got no patience for it. Precious little baby in a place like that." She stalked to her house and shooed the Dobermans in the back door.

Robin and Vincent stood for a moment in the welcome silence. "What's going to happen to her?" Robin said. "How long will you let her stay?"

"Long as she wants."

"That's generous of you." She couldn't keep the sarcasm out of her voice.

Vincent lifted his shopping bag and brushed snow from the bottom. "You have no reason to trust me," he said. "I understand. But I'm doing right here—you know yourself Dana needs help. I'm here, you're here, let's focus on that."

Robin watched as he walked onto the porch. She raised her hand in a half wave when Dana opened the door, but Dana was smiling at Vincent and didn't see her.

She got into her car and cranked the heat. Rattled, she misjudged the turn onto Burdock, jolted the front right tire over the curb. The thought of Vincent in that house was too terrible to consider. It hovered beyond her sightline, like snow-covered bushes hunched and hulking along the road. He didn't belong there. Didn't deserve to be there.

And he shouldn't be able to help Dana, to keep her and Emma warm and safe, chasing a redemption he didn't even know he sorely needed. Dana's words echoed— *some old guy*. Dismissive, unthreatened. Grateful.

Impossible.

Then a memory slipped in: paper bags of groceries at the Gleason Motor Lodge, in a room unfit for food. He'd tried, in his twisted way, to help her too.

*   *   *

She could skip the Landlord Association meeting. Without an urgent reason to go, all day she planned to stay home. East Green remained a disaster, and she had no way to rent out Dandelion Drive as long as they needed to live there. She had other things on her mind, and the landlords couldn't help with her escalating problems. And yet. Despite everything that had been happening, the memory of the photographs Vincent showed her lingered. The deer on his front lawn—there was violence there. A threat. Who knew what the men had planned or if they'd just carry on with childish pranks? But if they did damage—real damage—what would she do?

Robin couldn't wrap her head around it, but Dana needed Vincent. The house on Whistlestop Road was, despite everything, warm and safe. If Dana had any chance of getting on her feet and building a life, she'd need at least that much.

At seven that night, Robin drove to the Way Car not knowing what state the men would be in when she arrived.

Vengeance, it turned out, was in the air. Micheline had called Tom to announce that her gallery had received an angel investor: none other than Coketown Investments. Since she wasn't able to attend the meeting, the men were free to speak without anyone checking them. Robin, certainly, wasn't up to the job.

"What are these guys getting at, paying for *art*?" Ryan Snyder demanded. "What the hell is their game?"

"Micheline'll ruin them herself," Danny Hilson said. "Nothing but a money pit there."

The men fell into an uneasy silence. No one believed Danny. Robin could guess what they were imagining. She could almost see it, if she pushed aside her own history: downtown Four Points, suddenly transformed, the brick cheerful, the lawns maintained. Flowers, sculptures, beauty. More investors coming in, their repairs outpacing what the landlords could or wanted to afford. Their properties becoming a black spot on the town, their status endangered. The world, changing.

"Disrespectful is what it is," Tom said. The men leaned in, voices serious now, a beer glass knocked over and ignored.

"This is our town," Tom said. "Not theirs."

"We gotta keep going after the Cassatta," Snyder said. "That's their prize."

"Water main," Hilson said.

"Burn it down," Sam McConnell said, only half joking.

Tom held up a hand, acting as the voice of reason even as his mouth twisted with rage. "Only a matter of time," he said.

She met Tom's gaze briefly, then looked away. Tom Frost had a particular interest in driving Vincent from Four Points. If the other landlords discovered he'd pocketed $120K for Whistlestop Road—well, Robin could only imagine what fuel that would add to the fire. She slipped away from the table and went to the bar.

She slid onto a barstool. Beside her was a girl with pink-tipped hair, egregiously underage, her legs bare, dirty white boots in the neighboring man's lap. When the bartender brought the girl and man tequila shots, Robin asked for a glass of water.

"You can get water at home," a voice said in her ear. It belonged to a thin young man with a goatee, frizzy hair in a ponytail. He smiled, showing gray-shadowed teeth. "Bet Tanya here can do better than that."

He nodded to the bartender, who sent over a shot of vodka.

"Looks like water, don't it?"

"I should get back to my table," Robin said, but when she tried to stand, another man joined the first, standing so close that she was unable to slide off the stool. His hair was close cropped but hung to a V in back. A large tattoo—indecipherable gothic letters—covered the side of his neck. Robin scanned through the sea of bodies, trying to signal to the men for help, but if any of them saw what was happening, they looked away.

"That's Paul. I'm Shipler. Never seen you here before," the ponytailed man said.

"I'm with that group over there," Robin said.

The guys ignored her. "You gonna take that shot?" said Paul, the tattooed man. "Be a shame to waste it."

"You can have it," Robin said. "Here—buy another one too." She fished a ten out of her purse and laid it on the bar. "Have a good night."

They didn't move much but let her stand.

"Be that way," Paul called as she hurried to her table. "Just tryin' to be friendly."

Her stomach dropped when she found the landlords gone. They must have left through the back door. She exited through the back as well. The lot was almost empty. She could hear the Yough rushing across the street. She strode toward her car, only twenty feet away.

Paul and Shipler emerged from the shadows and blocked her path.

"Come on," Paul said. "Let's go to the river."

"I need to get home."

"Don't be that way," Shipler said. "You bought us drinks. That means you like us."

Paul stepped forward and took Robin by the elbow. "I said, let's go down to the river." His grip tightened as he pulled her across the parking lot. Robin's shoulder brushed his upper arm—it was massive, hard as a log. She tried to stay calm but couldn't stop her breath from coming in short, panicky gasps.

"Please," Robin whispered. "I think you have the wrong idea."

Paul jerked her forward again. "Over here," he said, leading her to a muddy incline that angled toward the water. "Not like you haven't done this a hundred times before, am I right?"

The moon over Shipler's shoulder was round and low. The men smelled of beer and cigarettes, but something else was there too—a metallic stench that chilled her throat and quieted her mind so that all she could think was, *Run.* But she couldn't run. Both men were gripping her elbows, pulling her down the muddy bank, the water bright with moon.

Then she heard, "Robin!"

Tom Frost was jogging across the parking lot, shouting her name, his heavy boots loud on the pavement. "Get the fuck away from her," he yelled. He had a shotgun in his hands, which he raised to his shoulder as he ran toward them.

"Fucking hell," Paul said. They shoved Robin and took off along the rocky shoreline.

Tom loped down the embankment and lifted Robin up. Her shoes were soaked, her pants covered in mud.

"They hurt you?" he said. His arm around her waist was strong. He wouldn't let her slip as he guided her to the road. The butt of his shotgun pressed into her lower back.

"I'm okay," Robin said, but she wasn't. She couldn't stop shaking, and she began hyperventilating, leaning hard into Tom.

"It's alright," he said. "You're alright now. You're alright."

He walked with her to the parking lot, sat her in the driver's seat of his Range Rover. She sank back into the cold leather and took a few deep breaths.

After a few minutes, Tom leaned in. "What the hell you leave for? Went to settle up, and Tanya said I better go after you. Said two guys followed you out."

"I looked for you. You were gone."

"Stopped upstairs."

"Who were they, Tom?"

"Who the fuck knows? Tanya says they're in there all the time, stirring things up. You don't go and sit at a bar like that—gives people the wrong idea."

"The wrong *idea*?"

"Sure." He patted her knee. "You alright to drive home?"

He walked her to her car and waited till she was buckled in with the engine running. Robin was so grateful, but suddenly anger—*the wrong idea*—boiled over.

"Why did you sell to Coketown?"

Tom stepped back. "Who told you?"

"You said you'd never sell. You said it wasn't worth any price to deal with Coketown."

"That house—it was going to be condemned," Tom said, "and my houses don't get condemned. So I made a deal. They did me a favor, taking it off my hands. I was protecting my financial interests. That's no one's business but mine."

"What happens if the other guys find out?"

"We're screwed—that's what happens. Coketown makes them offers like mine, they'll sell in a heartbeat. Last thing we need is Coketown buying more residential places."

"Because then things might get better," Robin muttered. "And we can't have that."

Her bitterness surprised her. She didn't want Vincent to be successful in whatever warped project he was undertaking. But nor did she want the landlords to continue as they always had, jealously guarding their degraded properties. She wanted—something else. She wanted to be able to breathe.

"You thinking about jumping ship on us?" Tom said. "Gonna take all that money you got and fix up some places?"

"Someone should," Robin said. "You know as well as I do."

"What I know." He didn't elaborate, just leaned close, forced a smile. "Get home safe," he said. "With Ray gone—"

He tapped the hood of her car and turned away.

She drove home with the heater blasting, never losing her chill. She tried to shake the sensation of walls closing in, of the strangers' two bodies cornering her, no escape. She pressed her foot on the accelerator, letting the buildings blur around her. The bends in the road came fast and frequent, but she knew them, could handle the turns. *Wrong idea.* For a long time, she'd believed she deserved whatever clawed its way to her, but she knew now it wasn't true. Terrible things had happened—she'd lost Ray, she'd lost their life together—but it wasn't her fault. None of it was her fault.

She slowed when she reached their neighborhood. The houses were spotty: one tidy and solid, the next one slumping on its foundation.

And her house—the one on Dandelion Drive. Its need for paint, its moldering front stoop. A reminder that she had never gone anywhere, that she was still rooted to Four Points, the place her son had died. This was her home again, at least for now, and she didn't have to settle for what Tom and the other men told her to. She couldn't keep punishing herself. Haley deserved better. The house was dark, the blue glow of the TV the only sign of life. Haley's presence seemed like a mirage.

A miracle. Blink, breathe, and, if she weren't careful, it would disappear.

CHAPTER 17

Robin's phone rang at 2:00 a.m. The violently buzzing vibration jolted her from her deep, dreaming sleep. She had a single clear thought as she reached for the phone, heart pounding: Haley was okay. She was sleeping beside her. Robin could feel warm breath on her arm.

"Hello?"

"Robin?"

"Yes."

"It's Dana. From Whistlestop Road?"

"Are you okay?"

"You said to call if I ever needed anything."

"Dana? What's going on?"

"Emma's burning up."

"Can you call 911?"

"No. No."

"Were you drinking?"

"What? No. I don't want the cops showing up here."

Robin was already out of bed, fumbling for a sweater to pull on with her leggings. "Sit tight. I'll be there soon."

She left without waking Haley.

Only one upstairs light was on when Robin got to Whistlestop Road. As soon as she slammed her car door, the Dobermans began barking from inside their house, the harsh sounds muted but guttural, threatening. She knocked, tried the door—open.

"Dana?" she called. The house smelled like the McDonald's wrappings littering the coffee table.

"Up here."

Dana was in Emma's room, cross-legged on the floor with Emma in her lap. Robin reached for the baby, a hot, limp bundle.

"She has a fever," Robin said. Unlike her body, her voice wasn't shaking. "Get me a cool washcloth and some Tylenol."

"Like, pills?"

"Infant Tylenol. It's liquid."

"I don't have that."

"Okay. Don't worry. I'm going to get some."

But returning this sick child to Dana was not something Robin could do. She called Cindy. "Robin? What the fuck?"

"Listen. I'm with Dana. Emma's sick. Can you bring over some infant Tylenol? A digital thermometer too?"

"I don't have any of that shit."

"Could you get it? Please, Cindy. Dana called me. I don't want to leave them alone."

"This is fucking insane." She slammed the phone down. But Robin knew she'd do it.

Robin, Dana, and Emma sat together on the floor, waiting for Cindy. Dana pressed a cool cloth to Emma's bare belly and back, rinsing it when it got too warm. The baby briefly opened her wet, glassy eyes to study Robin.

"I'm sorry," Dana said, more to Emma than Robin.

"Babies get sick," Robin said. "It's not your fault."

"I had her out yesterday. In the snow."

"Cold weather won't make her sick."

"I should've had that stuff—the Tylenol and thermometer. All moms do."

"It's alright, Dana."

"Was Haley ever sick? When she was a baby, I mean?"

"Of course."

"Sick as this?"

"Yes. Emma's going to be fine."

She was glad she hadn't told Dana about losing Trevor. It was a worst-nightmare story, more than a cautionary tale. Robin felt a quick pulse of resentment. She'd tried so hard, when she had Trevor, to do the right thing. She'd had a job, paid her rent, didn't traipse around town with an infant wrapped in blankets. She'd had infant Tylenol in the medicine cabinet.

"It will be okay," Robin said. "You were right to call me."

Downstairs, the door slammed.

"Yoo-hoo," Cindy called.

Emma's temperature was 103. High but not so high that they needed to rush her to the hospital. Cindy measured out the thick pink Tylenol and angled the syringe into the corner of Emma's mouth, pressing the liquid slowly into her puckering lips. Robin laid her back in the crib.

"Sleep," she told Dana. "We'll stay for a while and check on Emma before we go."

Downstairs, Cindy was unpacking a Walmart bag. "I brought food," she said. It was 3:30 a.m., but they sat in the brightly lit kitchen, eating chips and Nilla wafers straight from the packages. After fifteen minutes, Robin checked on Emma. Cooler, sleeping, her tiny breaths even. Cindy was drinking a beer when Robin returned to the kitchen.

"Want one?"

"Yeah."

Had she been alone, Robin would have made tea, but the cold beer was immediately what she wanted. She let out a breath she'd been holding since Dana called.

"Thanks for coming with that stuff," she said.

"Warned you about this—she's relying on you."

"You said she'd ask for money. She hasn't."

"Three a.m. house calls. Close enough. You got a kid at home."

"I told her she could call. I'm glad she did."

Cindy went to the kitchen window, loosened a corner of cardboard, lit a cigarette.

"Vincent's the owner," Robin blurted out.

"What?"

"The old guy letting Dana stay here. It's Vincent."

"Fuck's sake."

"You don't think—"

"No way," Cindy said. "Don't even go there. He's a fucking corpse, you know? Jesus. Get this guy out of our fucking lives already." She shuddered, blew smoke out the window.

"You can leave," Robin said. "Emma's fine."

"No. I can't." She took a few long drags on the cigarette, then stubbed it out on the windowsill, leaving a ring of ash. "We have to go down there." She lifted her chin toward the basement door.

"No way. No."

"What are you afraid of? More trash? More cat piss? Fuck it."

The basement door squeaked when Cindy pulled it open, its unevenly sanded bottom brushing against the floor. At these familiar sounds, Robin felt something shift in her body, an old injury suddenly inflamed.

"No," she said, but Cindy was already halfway down the stairs.

Robin followed.

The basement was smaller than Robin remembered, narrower and danker, the ceiling so low she could touch the ductwork. Some cardboard boxes were stacked at the farthest end. A broken laundry basket sat, collapsed, on top of the rusted dryer. Cindy took an agitated lap around the basement. Robin walked into the bathroom, with its old pink curtain. She turned the faucet on, ran her hands under the cold water. She smelled hair dye. She did. It wasn't a sensation trickling from her memory. The smell was in the porcelain bowl of the sink, trampled into the stained cement floor. It was in the walls, in the glass of the window. It was in the bent-up plastic stems of the fake flowers, stuffed into the jar. Robin felt a deep fuzziness in her temples: she was going to faint. She left the bathroom, sat on a wooden stair, and put her head between her legs.

"Are you fucking kidding me?"

Cindy was standing over her, feet apart, hands on her hips.

"I need a minute," Robin said. "It's the same down here. It's exactly the same."

"No shit."

"How long since you were here?"

"Christ. Thirteen years."

"It's not right. It should be different."

Cindy glared at Robin. "Bullshit. You thought it'd be exactly the same. This is exactly what you wanted—it's like a fucking *fossil*."

"I didn't want that. That's absurd."

The house settled a little. Cold air ribboned across the floor, then faded.

"Something I need to tell you," Cindy said. "About Trevor. The day he died." She was pale, trembling.

"The morning you left him here," Cindy said. "I told you I'd be home. I was home. I was home the whole time. But while you were gone I came down here with someone. Maybe ten minutes, fifteen tops. I went back upstairs after he left, and when you came home, Trevor was already dead."

"Did the guy—do something to him?"

"No. Jesus. No one knew he was there but me. Don't you get it, Robin? I was down here when he died. I had to be. If I'd been upstairs, I might've heard something. I might've got to him in time."

"You wouldn't have heard anything. I closed the door myself, so he'd keep sleeping."

"We were so fucked up, you know? We killed something, Robin. You and me. Even if every doctor in the world says it was a random fucking act of God. Crib death, SIDS, blah blah blah. You know what it is? Blood on my hands. That's all it fucking is."

"*Your* hands? I'm the one who left him there—"

Cindy cut her off. "This is why I didn't go to the funeral. Wasn't my place to be there in the church. Then you left town, and I never had to fucking say anything to anybody. I always felt like I got away with something. I hated that. Hated myself." Across her forehead, three deep wrinkles casted their own shadows. A cleft as deep as the side of a penny divided the space between her brows.

Robin wiped her eyes. "Why are you telling me this?"

"Because you fucked it up, coming back here, getting mixed up with Dana. I was going to hell, I knew it, I'd made my peace. Nothing I could do changed that ticket. I wanted it. It's what I deserve. And now—" She pressed her hand against the wall. She couldn't stand any more than Robin could.

"Where the hell'd this girl come from? Asking us for help, pulling us back here. I don't buy this shit, Robin, you know I don't, forgiveness and redemption and all that. Let me go to hell. I don't want to make it right. Nothing can be right in this fucking house, this fucking town. I made my peace, I had my daughter, I was happy." She covered her eyes with her palms.

"Dana's just a girl," Robin said, though she did not believe it herself. "She needs help."

Cindy took a ragged breath. "Fuck it." She climbed back up the stairs.

Alone, Robin put her arms on her knees, lowered her head, and cried. These tears were welcome and tinted with relief. She still blamed herself. She still blamed Vincent. Yet knowing that Cindy blamed herself too—that for decades another woman had lived with this dark remorse—lifted the weight from Robin's chest. Not entirely. The deep, anchoring grief was still enough to sink her. But she found she could lift her head above it, breathe through—and then stop, easily—the crying.

After a few minutes Robin steadied herself. She joined Cindy upstairs to clean the kitchen and went home.

CHAPTER 18

A roofing disaster at Deirdre's wiped out the third week of March. Melting snow leaked through the chimney flashings, and water pooled into one of the bedrooms. The paint on the ceiling was bubbled and peeling. A brown stain leached halfway down the wall. Robin hired a roofer, a painter. She stuffed their bills into a drawer and paid for materials with her high-interest credit card.

"Oh God, I'm so sorry, so *sorry*," Deirdre said each day, popping in to survey the progress when she got home from her shift. Then she pointed to a corner of the bedroom, a drip of white paint. "Hon? You'll make sure you smooth that out?"

Repainting was generous, well beyond anything Robin could comfortably do. A few hundred dollars, a thousand, didn't make a difference anymore. Robin didn't have anything, so she might as well make Deirdre happy, be a good person if not a solvent one.

The spreadsheet was a gunshot wound, red splattered across rows and columns like a deer's blood in the back of a pickup. Robin's wing-and-a-prayer methods were no longer working, if they ever had. She needed money, steady cash. Mornings, she woke with money on the brain, just as she had when her income was tens and twenties from the men, ones and change from her tables and booths and bar seats. Those stacks had grown so quickly. A night could add an inch.

Back then, the bills never added up to what they should have. Fifty when she felt she'd earned a hundred; a hundred when she felt she'd earned a million, enough to last the rest of her life. She imagined herself wandering around with her hands outstretched, always hoping that a strange man would see fit to smile on her. She couldn't do that anymore. The only possibility was to fix the wreck at East Green, for good this time.

She chose Cindy's lane when she collected supplies at Walmart. The woman in front of Robin was paying for her on-sale towels with ones and quarters—a waitress. Robin recognized the sensible black shoes, the trace of dried ketchup on the side of her hand. Cindy didn't bother counting or straightening the bills before shoving them into her cash drawer.

"Alright. Thanks," she said. She spun the bag rack so the woman could claim her towels, pantyhose, Chap-Stick, Suave shampoo.

Cindy glanced at Robin's items. Five packages of sponges, three bottles of 409, a couple of cans of Comet, Windex, Brillo pads, and carpet cleaner.

"What are you, a fucking Merry Maid?" Cindy said as she scanned the products. "For fuck's sake," Cindy said as Robin looked down. "Here, have an employee discount." She waved her badge in Robin's face.

"East Green," Robin said. "I need to rent it. I'm drowning. I can't buy what I really need, so I have all this." She waved her hand over the bottles and packages. "I don't know how to do anything I need to do. You've seen how it is there."

"Ray was a construction guy, right? He teach you anything?"

"I wish."

"Too bad. Now me, I know more than you'd think."

"Good for you."

"I'm saying I'll help you, alright? Don't want a fucking suicide on my conscience. Got enough there already."

"You'll help me? Are you serious? I can pay you, if you want."

"Like hell you can," Cindy said. "Don't matter. This is what friends do, right? We help squatters and renovate each other's rentals. Let's go to the mall later and get best-friends-forever charms." She gave the bag rack a violent spin.

The next morning, Robin watched out the East Green window for Cindy. Instead of Cindy's car, a banged-up pickup pulled to the curb. The truck bed was piled with cans of paint, buckets of plaster. Cindy was in the passenger seat, but the glare from the sun obscured the driver's face. When the doors opened, Cindy's old boyfriend Clyde climbed out of the truck.

"Clyde's gonna join us," Cindy said when she reached the apartment. "Don't look it, but he's a handy fucker." She shrugged at Robin. "He wants to help. And fuck if we don't need some help today."

In daylight, Clyde was scrawny and sallow, swimming inside a heavy camouflage hunting coat, a narrow mouse-colored ponytail sticking out from his John Deere hat.

"Hey," he said through a mouthful of chew. He worked it to the front of his teeth and spit it into a can he'd brought with him. "We'll trash the lino first. Then plaster and paint. What a fucking mess."

Robin turned to Cindy. "Cindy, I'm not sure about this. Tom Frost has a painter—"

"I'm Tom Frost's painter," Clyde said easily. "Whoever the hell Tom Frost is."

Cindy put a moist, warm hand on Robin's cheek. "Clyde looks like a piece of shit," she said, "and he is. But he's also a fucking great builder. I'm helping you out here, okay? Trust me."

Robin was surprised to realize that she did.

They worked all afternoon. Robin already knew how to peel the linoleum, and when it came time for the dry-wall repairs, Clyde showed her how to cut and hang the new sheets.

"Don't take much skill," Clyde said. "You'll need somebody who knows what he's doing with the plaster."

"He's talking about himself," Cindy said over her shoulder.

Haley and Amber came over after school and did their homework in the hallway. The Trundel brothers stopped by after their shift and checked out the progress.

"Solid," Damien said to Clyde, grabbing a sander to help him smooth the plaster. "Might have to upgrade," he said. "Naw, I'm kidding. Might have a cousin interested, though."

"Seriously?"

"Been in some trouble, but he's a good kid. Right, Kev?"

"We'll keep him straight," Kevin said. "Won't let him do nothing to your place, no worries."

Somehow Robin believed this too.

According to Clyde, three days of work remained: a day for painting, a day for flooring, a day for final touches like hanging the kitchen cabinet doors. If the Trundels were right about their cousin moving in, Robin was a week or two away from having a rent roll that would pay the bills and then some. She felt giddy, even though she'd maxed out two credit cards paying for new window panes at Cindy's and the materials Clyde kept hauling into East Green. She still had to figure out how to manage Dandelion Drive. It would be a balancing act, but she'd do it. Maybe when the ground thawed, she'd fix the lawns a little, make the places less of a blight on their neighborhoods.

No. She had to remind herself: in spring, they'd be back in Mount Rynda.

Robin's phone chirped while she was getting ready to scour the toilet. She'd shaken in half a canister of Comet in a thick mint-green layer, and she was letting it sit a minute—the idea of hitting her knees, bending over the yellow-stained porcelain, feeling strangers' scum wedge under her fingernails despite her extra-large pad of steel wool, threatened to undo her good spirits.

A text from Steph.

Are you looking for an apartment?

Robin's breath caught. She expected to be excited— she *was* excited, of course she was—but all she could feel was the pounding of her heart.

Mount Rynda?

In the old neighborhood. Myrtle Street. Studio unit over a garage.

I'll let you know, Robin replied.

A garage. Sharing a sofa bed in an apartment meant for a boomerang child or college student? In sight of her old neighbors? She wanted to go back, but not like that. Surely she could do better. She was capable of more than she'd been before. Robin flushed the toilet, letting the bleach wash away the grime. That alone seemed to prove her point.

Outside the bathroom, she heard Clyde return with pizzas, the activity of a hungry crowd. She'd think more about Steph's text later. She should get back out there and eat.

*　　*　　*

Cindy and Robin left East Green together. They stuffed the empty pizza boxes, two-liters, paper cups, and napkins into a garbage bag. Then they gathered their coats and stood at the door, assessing the work they'd done.

"It'll be real nice," Cindy said. "Have to say, didn't think you'd pull it off."

A weight had lifted. Robin could breathe. More work remained, but East Green had been tamed. Gratitude toward Cindy, toward everyone, rippled through her.

"Why'd you help me?" Robin asked. "You, Clyde, the others—I can't pay anyone. I don't understand why you're here."

"Our work not good enough for you?"

"I didn't mean it like that."

"I'm fucking with you."

"I'm serious, Cindy. You don't owe me anything. What are you doing here?"

Cindy tapped out a cigarette and tucked it under the edge of her navy knit cap. "You kill me. Even after all this you don't get it." She jammed her arms through the sleeves of her jacket. "Fuck it, Robin. You needed help, I helped."

"I didn't ask for that."

"Side benefit of coming home." Cindy grinned in a way that said she knew the word would chafe. *Home.*

After Cindy left, Robin turned off the lights and dragged the garbage bags into the hallway. Clyde had fixed the hinges and changed the dead bolt, allowing Robin to lock the door for the first time. She kept coming back to Cindy's words: *You needed help, I helped; side benefit of coming home.* How would her life be different if Cindy had been around in the months after Ray died? When things started falling apart, her neighbors in Mount Rynda, outside of Steph, having retreated completely? No one had helped her pack. No one had stored her boxes in their garage. No one had offered a minivan or a husband or a teenage son to help bring large pieces to storage.

Cindy would have dragged Clyde over with his pickup and a six-pack.

It didn't matter now. Robin would have sliced off her hand before asking Steph or any of the Mount Rynda women for that kind of help, so it was just as well they'd stepped aside. When Robin returned, she wouldn't feel indebted. The women could brush away their pity, having steered clear of its grit and stench.

*　　*　　*

Haley went to bed early that night, mumbling a goodnight to Robin. It was snowing again, great flakes that blew in sudden gusts against the house. A snowstorm could bring countless problems: frozen pipes, downed tree limbs, basements flooded with snowmelt. Someone slipping on an unshoveled sidewalk and suing her—ruining her. She'd have to go out in the morning to clear her property and make sure the tenants had cleared theirs. As the wind rushed and whistled, she opened an I.C. Light and drank half in three deep swallows. She never drank beer in Mount Rynda, but beer was all she could afford and exactly what she needed. She drank straight from the can and didn't worry about the ring it left on the plastic coffee table.

On a night like this, her neighbors on Dandelion Drive would be holed up at home, their cars slowly disappearing under lumpy drifts of snow. If she looked out the window, she'd see lights in each house, the blue glow of TVs. She didn't look. She let herself sit, alone—a familiar practice. Each day in Mount Rynda had been the same for herself and a handful of other stay-at-home mothers, the only living souls on Meadowbrook Court after 8:30 a.m. Robin had her activities, her standing lunch dates and weekly shopping trips and a flurry of PTA work, but many of the seven hours until

Haley got home remained unfilled. Robin would prep dinner, drink coffee, tidy up, vacuum. Occasionally a woman would jog down the street, ponytail swinging against a strappy Lululemon tank. Sometimes Robin would spot a young mother pushing a stroller. Each day, unease vibrated underneath the solitude and comfort.

What Robin felt tonight was peace. Her phone was quiet, the door was locked. Her muscles ached from lugging the ruined, rolled-up carpet—she'd heaved it herself into the bed of Clyde's truck. She'd worked out the budget and for the past three months had kept Haley and herself fed and sheltered. She hadn't felt so competent, so industrious, since she was seventeen, doing whatever it took to make sure she never went back to her mother's trailer. She was young enough then to be fueled by determination, but she couldn't pretend that had anything to do with her motivation now. It was Haley, all Haley. Without her, Robin may have followed Ray into the Yough—long enough, at least, to get soggy and cold and irredeemably sad.

Her phone rang. Robin answered it without thinking to screen the Mount Rynda number.

"You don't have to tell me. The garage won't work," Steph announced. "Listen. Robin. I have another place, right outside of Mount Rynda. A little more money. But the school district is great for Haley. And it's not, you know."

Not Four Points. That didn't need to be said. And Steph wasn't the other women in Mount Rynda. She'd been here the whole time, waiting for Robin to get in touch.

"It's a mother-in-law suite. Basement, but it has great light. My cousin's going through a divorce. She needs the money."

"Steph, I don't know."

But why hesitate? Wasn't this everything she had been working toward? Wasn't this why she had East Green's grit under her nails?

"Just come see it with me," Steph said. "No pressure."

"Okay," Robin said. She didn't know why her heart was racing, like an animal caught in a trap.

*   *   *

April 1, another rent collection day. The Trundel brothers: paid. Cindy: paid. Deirdre: paid. Nothing from Sister Eileen but an early-morning voicemail assuring Robin that the diocese would have her money soon—her apology, if not her rent, always perfectly on time. Robin entered the numbers into her spreadsheet. She'd known what she could realistically expect, but the satisfaction of finally understanding her work didn't lessen the stinging resignation when the totals fell short again.

She held on to an unlikely beacon: East Green #3. The end was in sight. Long days of work had done the impossible. Clyde had painted the whole apartment with a pale Swiss Coffee, eggshell finish. Robin and Cindy had laid carpeting, back-breaking work. For the bedroom, Robin chose the plushest by-the-roll option Home Depot offered, a synthetic beige. As Robin unrolled it, Cindy followed with a staple gun, tacking the edges. Not professional but good enough. In the living room, same carpet, same process. New shelf paper in the cupboards, a lot of steel wool to clean the stove and sink, window coverings throughout the apartment. There was a lot to do, a lot of money to spend. But with the painted walls and softened floors, East Green #3 was finally a place someone might want—one day soon—to live.

When Robin arrived at Whistlestop Road with a bag of pepperoni rolls and donuts for Dana, she heard hammering on the second floor.

"A radiator started leaking last night," Dana said. "Vincent's replacing the valve." She took a donut from the bag. "Thanks," she said. "I get so hungry when I'm tired. Baby over there is sleeping right through it."

"Go lie down," Robin said. "I'll listen for Emma." She went upstairs.

Vincent was on his knees in the hallway outside Dana's bedroom—a wrench in his left hand, a hammer in his right—struggling to twist loose the steam valve. Beside him, a large metal tool box was splayed open.

"Hi," Robin said.

Vincent looked over his shoulder, his forehead beaded with sweat. "Grab a hold of this, will you?" he said, extending the hammer. "Now you hit it while I pull."

Robin hesitated, then took the hammer. Vincent gripped the wrench with both hands and strained to pull it toward him, his face reddening with effort. Robin dinged the valve gingerly at first, then gave a good hard whack. With a hiss of steam, the valve released. Vincent untwisted it until it came off in his hand.

"Thanks," he said, sitting back on his heels and wiping his face. "An easy fix when you don't have twenty years of old paint to deal with." He dug in his tool box for a new valve, swiftly screwed it on. "There," he said. "Fixed."

He noticed her hands, the scraped knuckles. "What happened?"

"It's fine," she said. "I was doing some work at one of my properties."

"What're you doing?"

"Removing old paint from some cabinet doors. My hand got in the way of the sandpaper."

"Try Klean-Strip. Takes it right off."

"It's done now," Robin said.

"Need some more help?"

The sincerity of the offer stopped the scoff in Robin's throat. "I have enough," she said.

"Well, you tell me if you need anything."

The radiator hissed as warmth floated into the room. Vincent began twisting duct tape around the feet, blocking the holes in the floor.

"Check the heat in Dana's room, will you? Open the radiator the whole way."

Robin padded into Dana's room and bent to open the radiator valve. A sparkle caught her eye in the corner. Something sequined, peeking from the mouth of a large bag of clothes. Without thinking she rifled through— five pieces of clothing from Bon-Ton, all with tags. When Dana appeared in the doorway, Robin didn't bother to apologize.

"What are these?"

"Clothes from my friend Jaclynia."

"This Jaclynia—she gave them to you?"

"Yeah."

"Where'd she get them?"

Dana shrugged. "At the mall."

"These are forty-dollar shirts, Dana. Where'd she get that kind of money?"

Dana picked at a thread on her cuff.

"Dana? Did Jaclynia steal these clothes?"

"No! No. I don't know. She said she wanted me to have them."

Robin struggled to control her voice. "It's not as simple as that. Jaclynia will be in serious trouble if she gets caught."

"I told you, I don't know how she gets them."

"If she gets caught and tells them she's been giving you the clothes, you could be in trouble too."

"I'm fine."

"You've already had some threats about CPS, haven't you?"

Dana was silent.

"Think about what you're doing," Robin said. "Think about what's at stake. I can't be around all the time. I'm going back to Mount Rynda soon—you'll be on your own."

Downstairs, Emma shrilled, and Dana slipped away.

Vincent appeared in the bedroom doorway. "Heat's working fine," he said.

"Good," Robin said. "I need to get going."

"I'll walk out with you," Vincent said. "Need to ask you something."

Outside, Vincent stood in front of Robin's car door.

"What do you want?" she said.

"I heard what you said to Dana."

"And?"

"You can't leave."

Robin tried to open her door, but Vincent didn't move.

"You're needed here. You have a responsibility to Dana."

"This was always the plan," she said. "I need to get my daughter home."

Vincent kept his eyes on hers. "You belong here."

Fury washed over Robin. "How dare you tell me where I belong," she said. "And how dare you stand there and talk about responsibilities."

"I regret it," Vincent said. "I regret leaving you like I did. Are you using that as justification for leaving her?"

"I'm not *leaving her*," Robin said. "I barely know her. I'm doing what I can, which isn't much. She's got a place to live, you bring her food, she'll be alright. She doesn't need me."

"You don't know what she's up against," he said. "She's trying to do the right thing. She needs help."

"I know exactly what she's up against," Robin said. "And let me tell you, she's better off than I ever was."

"You moved on. Turned your life around. Your mistakes—ours—you got past them. Imagine what it would have been like if you'd had the baby. Dana's swimming upstream."

Your mistakes. Ours. As though Trevor were an ill-advised purchase.

"I took your money," Robin said quietly. "Remember that day? You gave me five hundred dollars and told me to 'take care of it.' You assumed an abortion was what I wanted too." She wouldn't look at him. From where she stood, she couldn't see the Yough, but she could hear it roaring. "I took your money, but I kept the baby. His name was Trevor." She stopped, waited for the sky to fall. When it didn't, she went on. "He was beautiful. He had your eyes. I loved him so much, and I knew you'd want to meet him. I thought you'd change your mind."

"Robin."

"This is where he died. This house." Robin felt bitter adrenaline rise in her mouth. "I just thought he was cold. There was never enough heat. We never had anything. You had whatever you wanted, whenever you wanted, and we had nothing."

Vincent didn't move. He looked past her, toward the river, toward the train tracks, his face white and stricken. "Surely you're not blaming me," he said in a low voice.

"Blaming you? *You*? Don't make yourself that important. It was me. *My* fault. This house—this town—nothing good can happen here. My life ended in Four Points. So don't tell me I belong here, that I'm needed here, that I have to stay. I can't." Her voice caught. "I'm sick about Dana. Sick. But I have Haley, my beautiful child, and I will do whatever I have to do to keep her safe. She isn't safe here. No one is."

She reached for the door handle. This time, Vincent didn't stop her.

CHAPTER 19

Empty. The inside of her body had been scraped raw and clear, holding little more than sadness and dry, frozen air. She wanted to snatch her secret back, but it just drifted in front of her face. She still was not free.

Robin was supposed to meet Steph at the Mount Rynda apartment that evening. She couldn't turn up empty handed, not after everything Steph had given her. To do so would make her a charity case, and she couldn't be that anymore.

Wine might have made more sense, a quick thank you. But wine didn't take time, and she needed to take time. She couldn't bear to sit still. At one point—it seemed so long ago—she'd been famous for her curried quinoa salad, brought to every potluck, made for every homey sit-down dinner. Steph liked it, she remembered. Robin went to the Shop 'n Save and yanked a cart from the tangled line. The salad required a lot of ingredients, which made Robin anxious. First, the produce section. She'd swap the heirloom cherry tomatoes for whatever was cheapest, which turned out to be a clamshell container of wrinkly grape tomatoes nearing its sell-by date. There was no kale or arugula, but baby spinach would do. She found a red onion, a red pepper, a wilting bunch of parsley, a bag of dried cranberries. Good enough. She usually soaked and cooked her own beans, but she didn't have time for that today, so she picked a can of Great Northerns. She selected the tiniest bottle of store-brand olive oil she could find and a small jar of peanuts instead of almonds. She balked at the price of curry powder, but there was no way around that. She searched for quinoa. Twice she walked the length of the rice-and-pasta aisle. No quinoa. No farro or bulgur either. No ancient grains. Brown rice was a questionable substitute but the only one available.

Her bill came to $45.26.

"I'm sorry, could I see the items?" Robin asked, angling closer to the cashier's screen. It wasn't any one thing, though the curry powder was a painful $4.39, the peanuts another $2.50. She paid in cash.

Back on Dandelion Drive, she spread everything on the counter, then sat in a chair and stared. She needed to boil water for the rice, wash and sliver the spinach, finely chop the vegetables. She needed to put the salad together so the flavors could blend, soak up the olive oil and salt.

She put on the water, rinsed the spinach, dropped handfuls of chopped onion and pepper into a large mixing bowl. When the rice was boiling, she forced herself to watch, the bubbles lifting the grains to the surface, spinning them, pushing them back under until the tough, dry rice was soft enough to chew.

Haley came into the kitchen while Robin was fluffing the cooked rice. She shook peanuts from the jar into her hand.

"Smells good," she said.

"My curried salad."

"For what?"

"For Steph. We're going to look at an apartment."

"Oh," Haley said.

"For us," Robin said.

Whatever response she had expected from Haley—Relief? Elation?—she didn't get it.

"Steph needs a salad?"

"It's a thank you for everything she's done for us."

Haley shook out more peanuts. Robin stopped herself from protesting, though she needed them for the salad.

"Do you want to come look at the apartment?" Robin said. "It could be our new place."

Haley's fingers wrapped around the counter and squeezed. "I'm hanging out with Amber."

Robin nodded. She focused on the positive: what mattered was that Haley had a friend. Teenagers were always going to be more interested in their friends than, say, apartment hunting.

"Planning anything fun?"

"Maybe the mall."

Robin was measuring tablespoons of olive oil. The important thing was to not make the salad soggy. Especially with the rice, which she'd already overcooked.

"Dana might come with us. Maybe one of her friends too."

"Dana?" said Robin. She scraped at the rice stuck to the bottom of the saucepan. "Is that a good idea?"

"Whatever." Haley rolled a leaf of baby spinach and bit it in half.

"I haven't washed that yet," Robin said. "Are you hungry? Do you want a green salad?"

"I'm fine." She rummaged in the bag of dried cranberries until Robin swept it away.

"Honey, I really need to let this sit," she said.

"Sorry, sorry."

Haley lingered in the kitchen.

"Everything okay?" Robin said, really turning toward Haley for the first time. Her hair had gotten too long and needed to be washed. She was biting the edge of her thumbnail, a nasty habit that had once led to an infection that left ripples in the nailbed.

"You should take a hot shower," Robin said. "You look tired. Maybe stay in tonight?"

"I'm fine. Don't worry about me." Haley smiled.

"Alright," Robin said. She jotted down the address of the apartment and left it on the counter. "I'll be back soon. Be good."

*   *   *

Robin left Four Points at five, the magical hour when the light over the mountains turned fiery and lit every branch on the maple-blanketed hills. The world was wet and weary, winter pulsing deep as blood, but in the pink sky and dripping ice from the bridges, she sensed spring. It really would come, softening those bristly mountains and coloring the sooty landscape of steel and coal. Another winter was breathing to a close, the longest, coldest, most godforsaken winter of her life.

She didn't believe it. A freeze this deep could never thaw. It had drained the color from the world and bleached the leftover bones. Any spring would be a false spring, painted garishly over desolation.

She made sure to leave a little extra time to drive past their old house. Not theirs. No longer theirs. The house that *had been* theirs. She turned onto Meadowbrook Court, eased off the gas as she stopped in front of number seventeen.

The house looked like a lifelong friend wearing unfamiliar clothes. On the front door hung a bright wreath of Easter eggs. To the left of the door was a red wooden bench lined with striped cushions. A nylon flag of tulips and daffodils waved in the breeze. The flag was Robin's—she'd ordered it two years ago from a Wayfair catalog. It must have been tucked away somewhere, in the basement or the garage. Would she be within her rights if she took it? It would fit into her handbag or under her coat. No. She'd leave it.

A light went on in an upstairs window, another, another. A timer. No one was actually home.

She pulled away from the curb, trying to shake off the feeling of dislocation. It was no longer her house, but Mount Rynda was still her home. The basement apartment was just on the other side of the municipal boundary, on the corner of a quiet cul-de-sac where all the ranch houses were a little newer and more anonymous than they were on the stately Mount Rynda streets. Steph's car was parked in front of the one with a basketball hoop affixed above the garage.

Steph met her at the driveway.

"I'm so glad you'll be around for my cousin," she said. "Not that it's, you know, part of the lease or anything, but I really don't think she should be alone."

The cousin was out late at a Girl Scout meeting—the kids were nine and ten, a little too young to be playmates for Haley, but they didn't make trouble. Not like Amber Sweeney. Not like Dana.

Steph had the key to the basement. She led Robin down the stairs into a small, neat garden with planting beds and a bench seat and to the designated entrance: 284 ½.

"They did this whole thing for his mother, isn't that depressing? She's got Alzheimer's, I think, but I guess that's his problem now. His and his paralegal's."

Steph rolled her eyes, the motion that signified that they were living in a suburban cliché. But a nice cliché, a safe one. So much better than any cliché Robin had ever been.

Inside, the apartment was remarkably sunny. Windows at shoulder height looked out over the garden. In spring and summer, they'd see green. The kitchen was no more than an alcove off the living room, a tight cave of cabinets, a sink, an oven, and a refrigerator, but the counters, amazingly, were granite, and the floors throughout the apartment were real wood. They'd managed enough space for one full bedroom and another bonus room. She and Haley could both have doors that closed.

"Really nice community on this street," Steph was saying. "There's a block party in the summer. I know, it's not Mount Rynda. But it's got to be better than where you are."

"It is better," Robin said, squeezing her hands into fists. "Of course it's better."

When the homeowner, Steph's cousin, got home and came down to meet her, she was polite but withdrawn. Now that Robin was a landlord herself, she could feel the cousin's appraisal of her seasons-old outfit, her scraped hands.

"It's a beautiful apartment," Robin said, willing admiration into her voice. "So cozy."

"I'll need a credit check plus the deposit to hold the place," the cousin said.

Robin could hear her voice wavering. Had Robin shaken like that her first time collecting rent?

"The credit check," Robin said. "Right. I thought Steph told you, I mean, everything that happened."

She saw the cousin's face fall. As hers would if a prospective tenant announced outright that they had bad credit, were struggling, were broke. Why did Robin feel relieved, thinking she wouldn't get the apartment? Wasn't this exactly what she wanted?

"Robin's had some difficulties since her husband passed," Steph said smoothly, consolingly. "But I can vouch for her. For anything. I'm insurance, Meg, okay?"

That was good enough for the cousin, who returned to the main house, pleased enough with Robin's promise to scan and send a copy of the full rental application.

"You hated it," Steph said. They were leaning against the hood of Robin's Highlander, passing the Tupperware full of salad back and forth, eating with plastic forks from Steph's glove compartment. Robin could barely swallow.

"Steph," Robin said. "It doesn't matter. I have to leave Four Points. I have to."

The more she said it, the less she believed. Robin had a gnawing dread, like she'd left the stove on at Dandelion Drive, only it wasn't just the stove. It was everything.

"Why do you have to leave?" Steph said. "Talk to me."

Robin took a deep breath. The words were waiting. *When I was very young, I had to do things I can't live with.* Telling Vincent about Trevor had opened the floodgates. She could speak.

"Alright," Robin said.

She started at the beginning, explaining what Ray had left her, the true state of the properties, why Four Points was impossible to bear. The blight, the landlords. Then she turned to the real pain: the poverty, the sex. Trevor. She told Steph everything. It felt good to let the words out. Talking lightened her. When she was done, there was silence. Steph had listened intently, not flinching even at the story's most unsavory, pathetic moments.

"God, Robin," Steph said.

"It's a lot," Robin said. "I know."

She had an urge to apologize—for herself, for everything she was and had been—but she squashed it. She wouldn't apologize for the life that had given her Trevor. She couldn't do that anymore.

Steph's eyes were on the main neighborhood road. Robin could hear a car slow and make the turn into the cul-de-sac.

"I had no idea," Steph said. "I wish—"

The car pulled up behind Steph's. The woman inside yanked the parking brake so forcefully that it squealed. The door flew open, and Cindy got out.

"Cindy," Robin said. "What are you doing here?"

"I've been trying to call you," Cindy said. "Where the fuck have you been?"

Robin glanced at her Highlander. Her cell phone, surely, was sitting on the seat.

"What's going on?" Steph said. "Robin, who is this?"

"Who am I?" Cindy stopped, looked around the cul-de-sac. Robin could remember the first time she really looked at houses like these, newly painted, the brickwork perfectly even. Cindy—in her Walmart winter coat, boots dripping Four Points mud onto the driveway—looked as out of place as a palm tree.

"Cindy Sweeney. I'm Robin's—I don't know what the hell you'd call me. It doesn't fucking matter." Cindy turned her attention to Robin. "The girls are in trouble."

Robin's gut cratered. "Haley?"

"Haley, Dana, Amber. The whole fucking crew."

Steph put a hand on Robin's arm.

"Oh my God. Is she okay?"

"She's fine. Upset but fine."

"Is she hurt? Is she in the hospital?"

"I *said* she's fine. I'll explain the rest soon. Let's go."

"Can I help?" Steph cut in, her eyes on Cindy. "I can drive, I can come with you, I can give you money, whatever you need—"

"All that's the least of our fucking problems," Cindy said. "But thanks. Really, thanks. This is way beyond what a nice gal like you can handle."

Steph didn't buckle. She squeezed Robin's arm, forced her to make eye contact. "Listen to me: call if you need anything. I'll be waiting. My phone'll be on all night."

"The weather's a fucking disaster," Cindy said. "Leave your car—I'll drive."

*   *   *

"Look at this place," Cindy said. Her sloppy K-turn spun her rear wheels onto a neighbor's soggy yard. "It's a real fucking shame you had to leave."

"Cindy. Please. Tell me what happened tonight."

They were approaching the Turnpike, the oversized colonials giving way to fast food restaurants, gas stations, motels.

"I'll tell you what happened," Cindy said. "I'll tell you because I was there, and you weren't."

"Don't do this. Don't put this on me."

Cindy stopped at the toll station, pulled a ticket free. She merged, accelerated, held steady at seventy-five. It was too fast for the conditions, but Robin didn't dare say a word.

"Where to start," Cindy said. "I guess I'll start when Amber called me from the jail." She glanced at Robin. "Do me a favor," she said. "Check your phone."

Seven missed calls, seven voicemails, six texts from Haley with a final one saying only CALL ME tacked to a string of worried-face emojis.

"You're moving back to the burbs, and the world's coming to a fucking end," Cindy said. If Robin hadn't known better, she might have missed the pain underneath the bitterness. But then Cindy's tone changed, any regret replaced by recrimination.

"So like two hours ago, I'm on break out back, having a smoke, so I answer when the phone rings. It's Amber, crying hysterically, fucking calling me from the mall jail. They're all there—Amber, Haley, Dana. Haley can't get ahold of you, and I'm the next choice. She needs me to come get them. So I go find Allison, that's the shift manager, and she gives me shit about taking off, even takes my card to make sure I clock out. Anyway. When I get to the mall, they've got these kids in a fucking holding cell. And by now they're a mess. The cop tells me I need to pay $387 in fines before they can go. 'You're fucking joking,' I says, and he says, 'The store's not pressing charges, they're lucky,' like we should be relieved. Apparently some other girl was the one they were after, and they'd taken her to the local precinct. So the girls are still crying, and Dana's like, 'I'll pay you back, Cindy, I swear to God.' And I says, 'You don't get it: I don't have that kind of fucking money.' That's when we called Vincent."

"Oh my God, Cindy."

"So Dana calls Vincent and basically says, 'It's me, your squatter, can you bring $400 to the mall jail?' And he fucking does. He walks in with an envelope full of cash, and right away the cops know who he is. Like he's a fucking movie star. He shakes a few hands, chats everyone up, then hands over the money, and we're outta there. Vincent wanted to get some dinner, but Dana wanted to put Emma down, so we go back to Whistlestop Road, and Vincent ordered a bunch of pizzas. The girls are freaking out, and that's when I decided to come out and fucking find you. No way you shouldn't be there. Fuck it, Robin." The story stalled as Cindy rubbed a hand over her eyes. "I had three girls and a baby under my watch tonight. It's too fucking much." She passed a Schwan's eighteen-wheeler, her tires slipping. The car fishtailed onto the shoulder, then straightened again. Her hands quivered.

"Pull over," Robin said. "Cindy. Now."

Cindy slammed on her flashers and cut over to the shoulder. The eighteen-wheeler blasted its low, angry horn. Robin undid her seatbelt.

"I'm driving. You're in no shape."

"What the fuck are you talking about, I'm—"

"I'm driving."

They switched. Robin hadn't worn shoes for snow, so the cold soaked into her flats as she hurried around the front of the car. It didn't matter. It felt good to be in control.

"Where's Haley now?" she asked when she'd eased back into traffic. She felt steady, practical. Shame, and the knowledge that she had failed her daughter, could come later.

"At Whistlestop Road with Vincent. They all are. Everyone under one fucking roof."

Every window was glowing when Robin finally pulled to the curb at Whistlestop Road. Vincent was on the porch, leaning on the railing with his hands clasped. He straightened when Cindy and Robin trudged up the steps.

"Here she is," Cindy called when she and Robin entered the kitchen. "Now we're complete."

Haley, Amber, and Dana were squeezed around the kitchen table, pizza boxes a barrier between them. Robin walked to Haley and wrapped her arms around her shoulders from behind, breathing in the fruity echo of her conditioner.

"Oh, Haley, thank God," she said. "I'm so sorry I wasn't here. I'm so sorry." She gathered herself. "Are you okay?"

"I called you, like, ten times."

"I'm sorry," Robin said. "But Haley, what were you thinking?"

Haley looked down at the table. Playing with her crust, shredding it, she might as well have been a toddler again.

"I'm sorry," Haley said. "But Mom, it wasn't my fault. I didn't know that girl was going to *steal*."

"You were there! You were all together. You should have known better. You should have known."

"I *said* I'm sorry." Robin wouldn't usually tolerate back talk, but she weakened at the tremor underneath Haley's defensive words. She kept her hands on Haley's shoulders.

"You know who's *really* sorry?" Cindy cut in. "Dana. Dana, why don't you tell Robin how sorry you are."

Dana put down her soda. "I'm sorry," she said. "Really."

"Tell Robin what you took."

"I didn't take anything."

"You helped. Same thing."

"Why are you asking if you already know?"

"I want Robin to hear it from you."

Dana said nothing.

"Okay, I'll remind you: six pairs of earrings, five silk shirts, a black cocktail dress. That sound about right?"

"Jaclynia took that stuff, I told you. She never even gave it to me."

Cindy ignored her. "A cocktail dress. This is the one that really kills me. Where you going, Dana? Fancy party coming up?"

Dana looked wounded. "It was so pretty," she said. "I just—wanted it." She sounded as young as Haley.

"Do you have any fucking clue what you've set in motion here? What you could lose?"

Robin put her hand on Dana's arm.

"Why didn't you ask us?" she said. "If you wanted something that badly? We've been trying to help you."

Dana's eyes were dry and bright. The mistakes of the day—the fear, the shock, the apologies required and apologies delivered—had pearled into scarcely contained anger.

"I should have *asked* you?" Dana said. "Asked *you*? Yinz don't have two nickels between you. Always bringing me stuff, giving me instructions like I don't know how to wash out a baby bottle. Like you know so much. Fine. You know more than me. But you don't own me. You can't tell me what to do. I don't need to *ask you*. And I'm not using Vincent for clothes and jewelry. I will *never* go as low as that."

She stared at Robin steadily, her eyes blending in with the twilight beyond the windows, and interpretation was blurry and impossible. The accusation was there. How much had Vincent told her? How much had she heard?

All Robin could do was steer the mess back to the baby. "You say you're so afraid of losing her," she said. "But doing what you did tonight—"

"You're trying to fuck it up," Cindy said. "Right? Fuck it up yourself before someone fucks it for you."

Dana scoffed. "That's crazy."

"This is it, okay? One more screw up, one more police visit, CPS moves in, and there ain't one fucking thing you can do."

"No one's taking Emma."

"You keep telling yourself that."

Emma started crying. Dana went upstairs without a word.

"Mom?" Haley said quietly. "Are they going to take Emma?"

"Nothing like that is going to happen," Robin said. But undefined danger suffused the room—as though anyone outside the house could come at any time and take something precious away.

Vincent didn't turn when Robin opened the door and walked onto the porch. She zipped her coat, pulled her scarf tight, and joined him at the railing, gazing, as he'd been, into the darkness. She'd never really grasped the size of the property until now, when she understood how to judge: easily a triple lot, the bulk of the house but also the vast plain of the yard dwarfing its neighbors.

"It's good you're back," Vincent said. "They needed you."

"I wouldn't have had the money to help. They needed *you*."

"I'm not talking about money."

"I'm sorry I wasn't here. I had no idea this would happen."

"No. But these girls rely on you. Dana, especially. You understand what she's facing."

"I barely know her. And I don't understand anything—I'm a cautionary tale."

Vincent was quiet for a long minute. The yard was silent, even the Dobermans next door were still.

"I was hoping you'd changed your mind," he said finally.

"About what?"

"Haley told me tonight that all you talk about is getting out of Four Points, going back to Mount Rynda. Her word was 'obsessed.'"

"She's thirteen," Robin said. "She's not meant to be here—Haley can't grow up in this place."

"So you still think leaving is best."

"I don't know what I think."

"Robin, do you believe in fate?"

Robin rubbed her eyes. Fate planned one true course. Her own life—there was no reason for any of it. There was no god or force or spirit that would have taken Trevor only to drag her right back to Four Points. It made no sense. It was punishment upon punishment. Why would fate waste its time?

Vincent palmed keys from his coat pocket. "There's more pizza inside," he said. "Eat something, if you're hungry."

Robin straightened. "Thank you for helping the girls tonight. And for Dana. For keeping this house—open for her."

"For all of you, tonight," he said simply. "Good night, Robin." He kept his distance as he passed.

Back inside, she went upstairs and knocked on Dana's door. "It's Robin," she said.

"It's not locked."

Dana was lying on her back. Her sweatpants gapped around the bowl of her stomach, the band held in place by craggy hipbones, not flesh. The long sleeves of her Steelers shirt were pulled tight in her crossed arms. She was staring at the ceiling.

"I guess you think I'm pretty fucked up."

Robin sat on the edge of the bed. "Emma's asleep?"

"She was kicking in her crib when I came up. Nightmare."

"Want to come back down? Eat a little more?"

Dana shook her head. "Cindy's so mad at me."

"I know."

"Why aren't you?"

She turned her head toward Robin, waiting. Robin *was* angry—wasn't she? Dana had been reckless. She had a baby to consider, a baby others had already threatened to take away. Today's shoplifting wasn't just a bit of teenage rebellion. No—there was no room for rebellion when you were trying to earn, day after day, the benefit of the doubt. So yes, Robin was angry because she was certain Dana had considered none of this. But she couldn't connect her anger to the ponytailed girl beside her, waiting for an answer.

"We make mistakes," Robin said. Her own odd, stilted words stopped her short. Not *we all make*, not *we've all made*, not *everyone makes*. We make. We. Women like us, people like us, but more specifically—you and I.

"We make mistakes, we make it right, we move on. You won't have to do it by yourself. What happened today—you have bigger things to think about. It isn't life or death."

It was, very much, a matter of life or death. People were punished for foolish mistakes, especially young girls like Dana, already teetering on the edge of something irreversible.

Even though Robin had survived this very truth, what would Dana gain from hearing it, besides a renewed awareness of doom? She messed up. She'd move on. She didn't need Robin hammering home the what ifs, the could haves. Dana was dealing with enough of those already. And the reality, which Robin was beginning to understand, was that what happened to Trevor most likely wouldn't happen to Emma. The same house, the same room, a young mother who could have been Robin herself—it didn't portend anything.

Instead, she reached over and put a hand on Dana's shoulder blade. "Sleep," she said. "Put today behind you. It's over."

Dana curled her body so that her head was on the pillow, her socked feet resting peacefully on the comforter. "Will you stay?" she asked quietly.

To sleep, and wake, in this house she knew so well. Listening to the night sounds she still heard in her dreams. With Haley—her strong, brave girl—in a room down the hall.

"Yes," Robin said. "I'll stay."

*   *   *

Robin couldn't fall asleep in the room where she had slept when she was seventeen. Too much was familiar. The chest of drawers that had held her clothes was angled in a corner. The walls were still paneled in faux wood, the ceiling the same off-white. Scrap plywood covered each glass pane. There would be no morning light, no familiar shadows at the edges of the walls. She wouldn't be able to see the bare branches of the sycamore at the side of the house. Those branches had been buoyant with palm-sized leaves when she'd lived here. Sun yellow in autumn, their edges curling and crunching as the weather cooled. A sound like home.

Haley, Amber, and Dana were asleep in the upstairs rooms, and Cindy was asleep on a couch downstairs. When Robin heard Emma stir—a brief, single cry—she realized she'd lain awake, waiting for it. Robin rose from bed and hurried down the hallway. She slipped into Emma's room and closed the door.

In the portable crib, Emma was quiet but writhing, sucking on her tiny fist. She arched her back but didn't scream when Robin lifted her into her arms.

"Shhh, shhh," Robin chanted, her hand on Emma's skull. Tiny, warm clouds of air tickled Robin's neck. She carried her downstairs, fixed a bottle of formula, and returned to Emma's room. There was nowhere to sit save a bare mattress on the floor, but the room was soothing, darkly warm. Robin settled herself on the mattress, back against the wall, Emma gulping the bottle. Her eyes reflected a bit of snowy light from a streetlamp far below. Air entered and left her lungs.

You're safe with me, Robin thought, but it wasn't true. No one could guarantee safety. No one could guarantee the continuance of breath.

The nipple of the bottle was slack and dripping against Emma's cheek. Robin put the bottle on the floor and tucked an afghan around her tiny body. Her arm ached from the weight of the child, but she didn't put her down. She was lucky to be here, keeping nighttime watch in this silent house. No other place could make her this complete, surrounded by the ghost of the son she'd lost and the living daughter she loved. Her life was not in Mount Rynda. Maybe it never had been. She'd found salvation there but a false salvation. She'd been forgiven for nothing and—despite the layers of lies she'd told herself—had left nothing behind.

And how could she be a good mother when she denied any sort of past? She was flawed. She was scarred. But, here, she was whole.

She stayed awake until a filmy gray dawn filtered through the snow clouds. She held the baby as long as she could. Then she placed her in the crib and returned to her own cold room to sleep.

CHAPTER 20

Robin rose at seven, before the others, and slipped downstairs to make breakfast in the kitchen where she once shared meals with Cindy and Rochelle. The Formica counter was cracked, the white metal cupboards shadowed where countless dirty hands had gripped the plastic knobs, but the kitchen was better appointed than her own on Dandelion Drive. Coffee maker, toaster, stocked fridge. Light filtered through the threadbare curtain. She toasted bread and scrambled eggs, mutilating them on the ruined pan she found in a cupboard, then covered the food with foil for when the rest woke. She put water into the coffeemaker, layered in a filter, measured coffee. Grounds floated on the brewed coffee like cloud cover. Robin skimmed them off with a spoon, drank two large mugs—draining the carafe—and ran it again with more water that puffed hotly in the heated well.

Someone knocked as the second pot dripped through. Robin unlocked the door. Vincent.

"Robin. What are you doing here?"

"Dana didn' t want to be alone last night. I stayed. We all did."

Robin felt almost dizzy in the thin light of morning, the coffee scarcely propping up a body that felt as flimsy and fragile as a paper gown. Vincent was flushed and stately, already in control of the day, carrying a cardboard tray of coffees—two—and a bag of donuts. He nodded at the food and coffee.

"I would've brought more. I didn't know."

Robin widened the door, but Vincent peered at her without moving inside.

"How was it for you, staying here?"

"I'm glad it's morning," she said. She couldn't tell him how her hips ached from lying awake for hours, how she'd listened for any sign or signal, how her heart had broken all over again when she understood that the only sound she would hear was the cry of another woman's baby.

These were things Vincent Latimer had no right to know.

Still, he'd saved them all last night. She wanted to offer something.

"I thought I'd visit the grave today," she said. The idea sprang up whole cloth, surprising her as much as Vincent. "Would you like to come?"

"His grave is here?" he said, then answered himself. "Of course. I hadn't thought. Which cemetery?"

"St. Theresa's. I haven't been there for twenty years— it's probably a mess."

"I'd like that," he said. "Thank you." He raised the coffee and donuts. "Let me put these inside."

She fished pen and paper from her purse to leave a note for Cindy and the others. She assured herself that it didn't matter if he visited Trevor's grave. It wasn't a private shrine or an urn tucked away in her home. Trevor's grave was a small pale-gray stone in a row of pale stones, in the open air, the hard facts of his short life—Trevor Nowak, Beloved Child, 1981–1982—gazing at the sky. She'd chosen a flat stone because she'd wanted him to see stars. She also couldn't afford anything else. That part of the cemetery might be decrepit by now, Trevor's stone covered over with two decades of grass and weeds. She knew Trevor's body was buried in a small wooden coffin someone picked out in the days after his death, but even when she was visiting the cemetery regularly— stopping by after her waitressing shifts, sometimes after midnight, when she could barely make out his name on the stone—she didn't feel him there. Instead, she felt him with her, deep in a womblike space he would never have to leave.

"Give me your keys," Vincent said outside. "I'll have someone retrieve your car later from Mount Rynda."

She handed them over, grateful for one less problem to solve.

"We'll take my car to the cemetery."

Robin clicked her seatbelt and stared straight ahead, trying to ignore Vincent's papery, spotted hands tightly gripping the wheel, the way he leaned forward a little to peer out at the road. If he was this old, then she was old too, but the equation didn't feel that simple. At forty-three and seventy-eight, they were a lifetime apart. Vincent eased along the freshly plowed winter roads. They said nothing to each other in the car.

The sun broke through the clouds, briefly, when Vincent turned into the cemetery. Robin directed him along the winding path. Where the land swelled, Robin stopped him.

"It's a beautiful spot," Vincent murmured. Robin didn't even think about responding.

They walked down the row to Trevor's gravestone. Small as a magazine, it reflected the sky. At first it didn't register that his stone was the only one legible. The others in this section were weed-shrouded, dirt-encrusted from spring after spring of muddy snowmelt. Trevor's had been shoveled clear and groomed precisely, the dead grass neatly edged, the small, built-in canister not full of rotten leaves and grime but a few recently wilted stems of cyclamen.

"Someone's been here," Robin said, surprised. She crouched and put her palm, briefly, on the stone, leaving a damp handprint that quickly faded.

"Not that many people knew him," she said quietly. "I was different after I had him. We kept to ourselves. It was better that way."

"Your parents?"

She shook her head. "My mother wasn't around. She was glad enough when she could put this behind her."

"What a gruesome thing to say."

"You wanted him dead before he was even born." Robin felt her chest open. She was free to say anything, lighter than she'd been in years.

She stayed crouched on the cold, hard ground a moment longer. Beyond her were the turrets of the Presbyterian church, the steeple of St. Theresa's, the Appalachian foothills rising at the edge of town. The Yough was visible below, lined with bare brown trees. Vincent was right: it was a beautiful spot. She should have been the one to keep his carved name clear, and she was grateful to whomever had taken it on. Wary too, unsure if it was a kindness she'd be expected to pay for.

She clasped her hands in her pockets and stood. She wanted to say a prayer—something simple, something she remembered the words to, *Glory be to the Father, and to the Son, and to the Holy Spirit*—but she didn't want Vincent to witness her making the sign of the cross.

"Are you ready?" she asked.

"I am."

In the car, Vincent put the heater on high but kept the car in park. "Thank you for showing me," he said after a few moments.

"You helped Haley last night. You had no reason to. I'm grateful."

"Robin."

Robin's pulse quickened. She fought an urge to jump from the car and run through the gravestones, straight to the road.

"I thought I might find you in Four Points," he said. "All these years. I just assumed you wouldn't leave."

"I did leave."

"I know," he said. "But when I came back, I looked for you. I kept looking for your long black hair. Anywhere new I went, I looked."

"What did you think would happen if you found me?"

"I didn't think that far. I just thought—maybe. Maybe you'd be here. Everything else was the same, so why not that too?"

"I haven't had black hair for twenty years."

"Here you are, anyway," he said softly. He turned more fully toward her. "I'm an old man," he said. "Almost eighty." He gave a small smile, inviting Robin to reciprocate, to acknowledge the unbelievable, relentless passing of years. Robin did not smile back.

"What I've done—" He shook his head. "You have to understand. You surprised me when you showed up at my house. You scared me. I've never forgiven myself, you see? Even before I knew what happened with Trevor, I regretted what I did to you. You were so young."

"Seventeen when we met."

"I was unhappy back then. I wanted so much more than I had."

"You had plenty."

"The wrong things. The wrong life. I chose badly."

"Does your wife know that?"

"I think so, yes. She left me and took our children. Not because of you," he added. "There were other problems. My anger. There was alcohol."

"So you paid a price."

"Not like you did. I see my kids and grandkids a couple times a year. But yes, I paid."

The heater blew warm air onto Robin's feet. For the length of a minute, two, Robin believed she would forgive him. She'd had her share of loss and heartbreak. Surely other losses, other heartbreaks, could change a person too. He smiled at her, puckers forming at the corners of his eyes. She slid across the front seat as though she were seventeen again and joining him eagerly in a rough-sheeted bed. He put his arm around her waist, gently, a confirmation of the time they'd had together.

"Please," he said, and he kissed her. Softly at first, then harder, his fingers tangling and pulling her hair. Robin didn't stop him. She leaned into it, touched his neck, his shoulders. She didn't know if anyone was watching, but let the people look. Let them see. She breathed him in, the same girl she used to be, holding on for dear life.

All at once Robin remembered why she'd spent so long being thankful for Vincent. Deep down, even after his series of rejections, she'd believed he saved her life. Over the course of their relationship, she'd stopped seeing men in Cindy's basement, pulling herself back from the brink of a too-imaginable life. And he'd given her Trevor, made her a mother, and once she was a mother, she had the strength dig in, get a better waitressing job, save her tips neatly stacked in a dresser drawer. She'd become a better version of herself—for Trevor and for him.

As she kissed him now, she could almost feel the way it used to be. She could almost feel how it was to love him. Maybe this was what he felt too, in the chilly car, within sight of Trevor's grave—how he himself once was: young. But he hadn't lived through what she had. For Robin, every memory was shadowed. Every terrible thing that had happened to her began with him.

She pulled back, slid over to her seat.

He wiped his mouth on his gloved hand, put the car in gear, and drove her back to Whistlestop Road.

Outside the house, Vincent turned to her. "What you told me, about Trevor—I'm glad I know."

"Glad?"

"I'll be burdened for the rest of my life. As you've been. It's a trick, not knowing the worst, thinking all along you're free." He cupped her jaw in his palm, leaned over, and kissed her, long and slow. "When can I see you again?"

Robin jerked away. "Are you insane?"

"I just thought—"

"We've both said what we needed to. That's it. Done, finished, over."

"It's not over. We have a history."

"And?"

"That means something. It matters to me."

"It *matters* to you?" The power he once had over her glimmered like frost on the glass. *It matters to me.* Once she would have sliced her own flesh to hear those words from Vincent Latimer.

"I'm old, Robin. I have the chance to make this right." He reached over, but Robin dodged his hand.

"There's still something between us," he said. "You can't deny that. We can start again, move on from here together. You can't pretend you haven't thought of it too."

Robin sat back. Vincent's car was an old Nissan sedan with fuzzy red-poly seats. There was dust on the dashboard. A small cloth bag had been affixed to the glovebox door with a silver nail, stuffed with crumpled tissues, a wrinkled receipt. The smell of Luden's cherry cough drops and powder-scented lotion sickened her. In an instant, Robin finally saw him—not as the monster who had ruined her life but as an old man trying to make his own peace with the past. What she felt wasn't exactly forgiveness. It was a distance behind her, a long stretch of road shadowed so deeply it had nearly disappeared, and she could no longer understand why she was still straining to see.

"Your properties," she said. "No one wants you here."

"Do you think I'm wrong to help?"

The question was earnest. Robin had a sense—strange, given how little care Vincent had ever given to her opinion—that he'd leave if she asked him. They both knew that the debt he owed her could never be repaid.

She shook her head. "Stand your ground."

"I'm not going anywhere."

He looked away. Robin, shaking, got out of the car.

CHAPTER 21

Late morning, Dandelion Drive. They'd left Dana settled, with promises to check in the next day, and piled into Cindy's car to go home. Cindy pulled to the curb, kept her foot on the brake, didn't even put the car in park.

Haley was in the back seat. After a low murmured exchange with Amber, she climbed out of the car and walked with slumped shoulders to the stoop.

"Thanks, Cindy," Robin said. She gripped the handle of her door. "I'll call you. We'll figure out what to do about Dana."

Cindy nodded. She pulled away from the curb as soon as Robin stepped clear.

Robin sifted out the keys and held the rattling screen door open with her hip as she unlocked the deadbolt and let them in. Dandelion Drive was no kind of home, but a breath she had been holding released when they stepped inside. Sun streamed through the broken venetian blinds, and Robin was finally overcome with the sick brightness of not having slept. She went into the bedroom, left the clothes she'd worn to Mount Rynda in a heap on the floor, and pulled on her softest flannel pajama pants and an old sweatshirt of Ray's. Haley was sitting on the couch when she returned, and Robin sat beside her.

"I want to tell you I'm sorry," she said. "For bringing you here and for the mess your father left us but mostly for last night. For leaving you like that. And not being there when you needed me."

"It's alright, Mom. We were stupid. We'll pay Vincent back. We'll figure it out."

"I'm not talking about the shoplifting."

Haley cocked her head, knowing that something was coming, but she couldn't know what. Robin had to do this. People knew now—Cindy, Vincent, Steph—and Haley had to be one of them.

"I made a lot of mistakes a long time ago," she said. "The kind you can't take back." Robin bit her lip, trying to think of how to proceed. "The point is that I shouldn't have left you, and I never will again."

Robin hesitated when Haley snuggled next to her.

"It's almost spring," Haley said.

"Yes."

"You said we'd be back in Mount Rynda by spring."

"I know. I'm sorry. This has been so much harder than I'd planned."

"So we're not going back."

"Not now. No."

The apartment Steph had found for her barely even entered her mind.

"I thought that was what you wanted."

"I did want it," Robin said. "More than anything. But it wouldn't be like it was before." She thought of the ease of their old life, their pot of worries so small it was like they'd been protected by a kind of enchantment.

"Not that anyone asked me," Haley said, "but I think we should stay here."

"You want to stay in Four Points?"

"I don't want to live where Dad was. Doing all the stuff we used to do together." They'd never been able to speak of Ray without crying, but this time Haley looked at Robin with dry, clear eyes. "We can find a nicer place to live here and just—stay."

"It's not that easy," Robin said.

"*Why*?" Haley said. "Couldn't you get a normal job here? And we could get a real bed? A real coffee table? Amber's lived here her whole life. Her mom—Cindy—grew up here. *You* grew up here."

Robin felt the weight of her secrets pressing down on her. Haley listed her reasons like staying was just that easy, as though because people she knew, and loved, were here, Four Points couldn't be that bad.

"Haley," she said. "I'm not—it's just hard."

And then Robin told her. She told Haley about living at Laurel Estates, about moving in with Cindy Sweeney and Rochelle, the rented room. About taking money for sex. The freedom it bought and the cost of it, the shame. She looked Haley in the eye when she told her because her daughter was smart, and savvy, and brave, and she understood. Robin told her about getting pregnant and losing her son. About meeting Ray and Robin's chance for a new life that fully eclipsed all the terrible things she'd been through.

She left out Vincent. Perhaps it was an acknowledgment that he would remain somewhere on the periphery of their lives, and she couldn't, ultimately, let Haley hate him.

The telling left Robin feeling spent. She breathed a heavy sigh, let her daughter see her exhaustion.

"It's never going to be easy like it was in Mount Rynda," Robin said. "There's too much history."

Haley hugged her. Lunged at her, really, all hard elbows and bony shoulders, loose strands from her ponytail pressing into Robin's mouth. Haley was so close now Robin could smell the Juicy Fruit gum on her breath, yesterday's Pantene conditioner on her scalp. She could smell Whistlestop Road in the fibers of her sweater and squeezed harder.

After another minute, Haley pulled away. She didn't meet Robin's eye. Across the room, a text chimed on Haley's phone, then two more.

"Amber," Haley said. "We were going to hang out."

"Go," Robin said, and Haley looked up, relieved.

"Get some air. But Haley—Amber doesn't know about all this. Cindy will tell Amber herself, when she's ready."

"I won't say anything," Haley promised. She rose from the couch but stopped before going for her phone. "So you and Cindy were, like, BFFs."

"I guess so. Yes."

"Just like me and Amber." She was working through something, Robin was certain, on the cusp of understanding the dangerous paths that beckoned. Then she said, "So weird," and picked up her phone and walked away like the teenager Robin had sacrificed everything to let her be.

*　　*　　*

Hard knocking startled Robin from an accidental nap. After last night, no good could come from a stranger at the door.

But on her doorstop was Steph Pacholski, in a turquoise, ultralight down coat and chestnut-brown Sorels. She carried three bags: a small shopping bag from Sephora, a plastic bag from Sheetz, and a paper sack from the Bowl & Jar Bakery. At the curb was her white Volvo SUV, glowing like a comet.

"You are not an easy person to find," Steph said in greeting. "I must have asked ten people at Sheetz before I found someone who knew you."

"What are you doing here? You didn't call—did you?" Robin hadn't checked her phone for hours.

"No," Steph shrugged. "You'd have told me not to come."

"You're right. I definitely would have said that. Steph—"

"I brought scones," Steph interrupted, holding up the bag from Bowl & Jar. "Your favorite, maple walnut. And coffee, if it didn't spill in my tote. Don't worry, it's in a Klean Kanteen—bought it two hours ago, and it'll still burn your tongue." Her face softened. "Please, Robin. I'm here. Let me in. I've been so worried."

Steph inhaled sharply when she stepped across the threshold. Robin had lived here for months, but the feeling of her own first glimpse rushed back. The old stained couch. The plastic coffee table. The sallow and sickly light streaming around the cardboard covering the cracked window panes.

Robin had known Steph for years. She knew Steph was struggling to conceal her shock, that she'd planned to stride in and take control with her usual bossy competence. Four Points had thrown her.

"Let me take your bags," Robin said.

Steph tried to collect herself. "The Sephora is for Haley," she said. "Just a little something. We can eat the scones now, if you have a plate—I mean, of course you have a plate." She laughed nervously. "And the other bag has two MTOs from Sheetz. Meatball sub and barbecue ham. They smelled amazing. I kind of want one now, actually. Forget about the scones."

In the kitchen, Steph hung her coat on the back of her chair. Robin cut the sandwiches in half and put one half of each on two plates.

"This is exactly what I want right now," Robin said, surprised by how hungry she suddenly was and how good the sandwiches looked.

"Me too."

For a few minutes they did nothing more than eat the sandwiches and drink the hot coffee Steph had brought. There was no reproach in the way Steph perched in the metal folding chair, legs folded lotus-style, just two girlfriends sharing a snack. She had been surprised by the state of the house, but the rest of it—Robin's past— might as well have been a light fixture on the ceiling, out of their sightline.

Steph sat back. "So. This is where you'll be."

Robin tried to come up with some sort of salve, an assurance that really, she was alright. "I think so."

Steph nodded. "We'll need to do something about those blinds, at least. That window. This furniture."

"The blinds are the least of my concerns," Robin said.

"Oh, Robin, I know that. But I need a way to help you, and blinds? I can do blinds."

She stood, gathering her coat, visibly relieved to have a project. "You remember Janna Plickett—her daughter was a year ahead of Haley? She shut down her interior decorating business last year and has a whole storage unit of décor samples she tries to unload on me every single time I see her. I can finally say yes. I can fill your entire living room with throw pillows." They were at the door. Steph fiddled for keys in her slouchy tote. "You can come up for lunch, and we'll have her take us to her unit," Steph said. "I'll call you next week. Will you pick up?"

"I'll pick up. Promise."

Framed in the doorway in her tailored coat, carefully pushing hair from her temples under the soft band of her cashmere hat, Steph looked like an exotic creature who'd taken the wrong fork in the road.

"Your Klean Kanteens," Robin said suddenly. "They're in the kitchen. Let me grab them."

"Forget it. Just bring them to lunch next week." Like they were neighbors accustomed to leaving things on each other's porches. As though the distance between them weren't so great.

"I will," Robin said.

When Steph was gone, Robin peeked in the Sephora bag she'd left for Haley: a rose-gold lip gloss from Rihanna's new line, three spice-colored nail polishes, and a handful of gel masks in foil packets. Haley would love them.

CHAPTER 22

The thick envelope came via FedEx, signature required. Only by luck was Robin home. She'd been halfway to Home Depot to buy a bulk roll of industrial-size trash bags when she remembered the grout she'd meant to return. If she was lucky, it'd turn out to be an even exchange, like shopping for free. She was home when FedEx rolled up, her purse on her shoulder, her coat buttoned. Caught up in the momentum of her errand, she nearly tossed the envelope aside. It was marked PRIORITY OVERNIGHT, heavy enough to give her pause. She glimpsed at the sender: Dunson & Carew, Attorneys at Law. She set down her purse.

The subject line read: *Re: Warranty Deed to 1 Whistlestop Road.* She read the brief note from the lawyer. *Please find enclosed the Warranty Deed to 1 Whistlestop Road, signed by Vincent R. Latimer and notarized by our office. This is a legal and binding deed transfer and will be recorded with the county registrar. Please sign where indicated in the presence of a notary and return the deed to us at your earliest convenience.* She read the entire packet of papers, sitting on the edge of the couch, in her coat, by the door. By the time she flipped the final page, she understood: Vincent Latimer was relinquishing his ownership of the house on

Whistlestop Road. If Robin signed these papers, the house would be hers. It was not a sale. Robin owed Vincent nothing. He was simply—giving it to her.

There had been a misunderstanding.

She called Vincent. "What are you doing?"

"You got the papers."

"I read them, but I don't understand."

"The process is clear cut. There will be tax implications, but right now all you need to do is sign. There's a clause about legal expenses. Those will be covered. You can develop the property as you wish."

"Is this a joke?"

"Those are legal documents, Robin. Take them to your own lawyer if you want, but it's not complicated. It's a gift, is what it comes down to. A burden, maybe, considering the state it's in, but a gift."

"I can't accept a gift like that."

"It's already done. You just need to sign."

An idea stopped her cold: what he might want, what he might ask. The demands were almost limitless. "Why are you doing this?"

"I would never have bought that house if I'd known what happened there. It's always belonged to you, hasn't it? Has any other place in the world meant as much?"

Robin couldn't answer.

"I don't have your exact numbers," Vincent went on, "but I can guess you'll benefit if you can rent out your place on Dandelion Drive."

"You're not suggesting I *live* in that house."

"It's your decision. I think it'll make things easier for you. Let me be clear: someday, with enough work and enough change in town, it could have significant value. That's years away, understand, with major restoration. But money like this is why I'm in Four Points—there's opportunity here, if you go at it right. It's a beautiful house. Good bones."

"What about Dana?"

"She stays, of course. She stays with you."

For a long moment, they were silent.

"Think about it, Robin," Vincent finally said. "I want you to say yes, but I want you to be sure."

Robin couldn't speak. It was too clear: she would rebuild her Four Points life piece by piece from whatever remained. The basement on Whistlestop Road, the train tracks, the Rowdy Buck, the room where Trevor died, the ambulance that took his body, all those ghosts. Was she sure, Vincent wanted to know—was she sure—

"Yes," she said. "I'm sure."

A darkness parted in her mind, finally revealing the months and years ahead. Even in Mount Rynda, during the happiest days with Ray in their beautiful home, preparing a gourmet meal for their well-dressed friends, Robin could barely see to the end of the evening, let alone to the end of her life. Her view was blocked by too many secrets, too much guilt. Go back to Mount Rynda—for what? For a basement apartment, private school tuition out of reach, holding on to the tenuous threads of a life that had always felt unreal? *For what?* Now—from the turret room at the top of the house on Whistlestop Road—she'd be able to see the mountains. She'd see the sun glint on the river.

She folded the papers into the pre-addressed and pre-stamped envelope. She tucked the envelope into her purse, put on her coat, and retrieved the grout from the porch. She'd sign the papers before the library's notary on the way to Home Depot.

The house on Whistlestop Road was hers. In some ways, it always had been. The years between departure and return hadn't been salvation but a long-held breath she'd always been destined to release.

CHAPTER 23 (SPRING)

Every day, Clyde Ellwood wore a white-ribbed tank top and jeans that hung halfway off his hips. A cracked vinyl belt—the same one he'd used on the windows of 1118 ½ so many months ago—kept the jeans from falling off entirely. He arrived each day at Whistlestop Road with a doubled-up plastic grocery bag heavy with tools. Old plastic Coke bottles, knifed in half and arranged in a milk crate, held his screws and nails. He came at odd, irregular hours—sometimes eight in the morning, sometimes three in the afternoon—and Cindy convinced Robin to give him a key. "Let him work how he works," Cindy said when Robin first mentioned his erratic schedule. "Clyde ain't the type to have a fucking day planner." He sometimes brought help, never introducing them. Robin often came home to a stranger or two on her porch, rifling through Clyde's cooler for an I.C. Light.

It wasn't how Ray used to work, with his punctual, professional team of licensed demo guys and cabinet guys and plumbers and electricians, his constantly buzzing smartphone keeping track of schedules and appointments. But somehow, Clyde was getting the work done. In the living room, he'd started ripping out botched, half-done drywall, preparing to insulate and then replace with fresh new walls. Two of his guys had started ripping out the toxic carpet and sanding whatever parts of the subfloor they could save. The rest—the crumbling, damp, rotting pieces—they would replace. Robin, Haley, and Dana were already picking paint samples and flipping through carpet books.

When the living room was finished, Clyde would replace the windows and go on to the kitchen once Robin had saved some cash. Four months, probably. Three, even, if no one had any major problems.

Scott Chatham had been surprised when she'd sent him the deed transfer to add to her files. He'd called immediately.

"I don't get it," he said.

"Another property. I'll need tax advice. I might need a HELOC too."

"You're staying?"

"I am."

"But if you have this other place now to rent," Scott said, his lawyerly reasoning firm, "you'll have enough money to do what you wanted."

"Thanks," Robin said. "For all your help. I owe you one. Come visit me sometime—we'll go tubing down the Yough."

On May 1, a bright spring Saturday, Clyde arrived with a truck full of odd-sized boards and electric saws to rebuild some shelving in the entryway. The work was noisy, dusty, but the day was mild, so Robin sat on the porch with Haley, Dana, and Emma, who was zipped into a warm pink sweater with a hood that made her face as tiny as the chipmunks beginning to dart from their winter nests.

As usual, Deirdre Boone arrived first. "Water's leaking under the kitchen sink," she said. "And there's air in the pipes again. Nearly had a heart attack when the water spit out of the shower last night." A plumber, then, two hours max—peanuts compared to the last few months.

The Trundels came next, Damien and Kevin and their cousin Sean. After giving Robin their cash, they went inside. The noise of the circular saw stopped briefly. Robin heard Clyde explaining plans for the kitchen, hinting that he'd need some help if they were looking for extra work.

Robin breathed a sigh of relief when the new tenants, the ones renting Dandelion Drive, pulled up in a dented station wagon. Maureen and Lenny Honsaker and their five-year-old son, Kyle, walked together to the porch. Maureen kept her hand on Kyle's head as Lenny gave Robin the money.

"I wanted to ask about the yard," Maureen said. "Would you mind if I put in a little garden? Something outside the back door. I won't dig any of the grass."

"What will you plant?" Robin said.

"Summer things," Maureen said. "Potatoes, carrots, tomatoes, squash. Kyle wants pumpkins for Halloween." She peered beyond Robin, through the open door, out across the wide front lawn. "It's funny," she said. "I think I used to know someone who lived here, back when I was a kid. Someone my mom worked with when she was a waitress—there was a funeral, I think. Something bad."

Robin waited for the tidal force of memory, of discovery, but it didn't come. Only because a damp breeze rose off the river did she shiver. "Every house has stories," she said.

"I'm sure you've heard a lot, being a landlord."

"Sure," Robin said. "Here, let me help."

Kyle was teetering down Whistletop's stairs, and Robin held a hand out, steadying him.

Cindy had delivered her own rent earlier in the day, so when the Honsakers left, Robin counted the money, separating the bills into tidy stacks of a hundred. This wouldn't always happen. Even next month was uncertain. Sister Eileen had told Robin last week that the Romanian missionaries were finally moving on from Sacred Heart's religious housing, freeing a room for her and sending Robin into a new whirlwind of interviews and background checks. Plus, even tenants like the Honsakers and Deirdre, honest and good-intentioned, could find themselves, for endless reasons, out of cash, out of luck. She'd been there herself. Was still on the edge, might always be, as long as her livelihood was cleaved to boilers and shingles, sewage stacks and electric grids. Although now—with Haley content, Dana and Emma thriving with her help—she felt shielded from cataclysmic disaster. She should knock wood—she did, on the porch rail, discreetly—but finally, on the cusp of spring, she could feel her dread cracking with the thaw.

*   *   *

The opening of Micheline's gallery took place that night. The sunny afternoon had given way to a raw, chilly evening that felt more like winter than March had. The weather, however, didn't keep people away. At seven, a line stretched outside the gallery door, thirty or so curious men and women huddled on the sidewalk, their jackets hiding the care they'd taken with their outfits.

Robin pulled up right when the line began edging into the gallery. She was wearing a royal blue dress from another life—buttons down the back, little capped sleeves. She'd bought it when she and Ray had season tickets for the Pittsburgh Symphony. Beside her was Haley, in a purple skirt and purple bolero over a black leotard.

"Fucking heels," said Cindy, struggling to hoist herself from the back seat. But her voice was light, and her hair was pulled into a neat side braid secured with an elastic that matched the green-and-gold stripes of the tunic peeking from the bottom of her spring coat. Haley hurried ahead with Amber, in a stretchy black mini dress that was much too sultry for an eighth grader—but Robin's impulse to judge felt as light, as fleeting, as the mist dampening her shoulders.

The gallery was crowded but quiet as people gazed at the gold paint and glitter and looked curiously at the art. Robin scanned the room. Only strangers, so far. Micheline clicked over, her top eyelids lined with shimmery purple.

"Sign the guest book," she said. "Have some wine. People like it, you see? Already they like it."

Robin and Cindy each took a plastic cup of wine and began their own path around the walls. Dean Smith's dead cat in oils, the scattering of Jesus-faced stones, Connie Scant's watercolor sycamore, the livelier smashed windshield photos from Gary Butke's junkyard—in a crowd, in the evening, the art was real, respectable, something worth coming to see. When Steph came for a visit, Robin would bring her here.

Suddenly, someone laughed. "Hey, Micoy," a man called out. He was standing near some pencil drawings of Laurel Estates. "Ain't this your trailer? With them azaleas?" A few people joined him, then turned more attentively to the other art, searching for themselves, their neighbors, finding themselves in all of it.

Robin lingered by Dean Smith's cat when Cindy moved ahead to study the Jesus stones. A familiar face appeared—Tom Frost, frowning at the glitter-caked walls and turning his disapproving gaze to her. He edged closer.

"How's the new place working out?" he asked.

"It's a project, but it's coming."

"Heard you got Clyde Ellwood working."

"He does a good job."

"I know," Tom said. "I was going to tell you about him. Guess you're a step ahead of me." He pretended to study the art. "Have to say, I'm confused about how it went down," he said. "You and Latimer."

"You're the one who sold him that house," Robin said.

"That's different," Tom said. "That was business."

"This isn't?"

"No business I want any part of," he said.

It took a moment for Robin to understand. "You have it wrong," she said.

"Do I?"

"You can't possibly think—"

He laughed, glancing around to make sure they were still alone. "We know about you," he said quietly. "I just wanted to say that. You wanna team up with Latimer and shoot yourself in the foot—fine. You do that. Don't think that means you can act all high and mighty. We know what you did back then."

"It was an ugly time in my life."

"Sure as hell sounds like it."

"And I never asked for any of this."

"You said yes, didn't you?"

She met his eye.

"Yeah," said Tom. "So you get why people might talk."

"Let them talk," Robin said. "You can't scare me, Tom. Tell the others. Tell everyone."

Impulsively, she hugged him. He'd helped her, taught her—about landlording and the risk of blind trust. What could he say, what could any of them say? It was done, it was over. She'd spent years drowning in guilt, so intent on hiding her past she'd kept it close instead of letting go. Someone was tapping a wine glass. Micheline was going to speak.

Micheline was talking, raising her glass in tipsy thanks, drawing scattered cheers and applause. Robin stood at the back. Cindy joined her.

"You okay? Saw Tom giving you shit."

"He's angry."

"He'll get over it. You worried you ain't on the right side, after all this?"

"I know I'm on the right side," Robin said. She gently nudged Cindy with her elbow. "Right here next to my old friend Cindy."

"Bet you never saw that coming," said Cindy. She elbowed Robin back, harder. "I did, though."

Her voice invited the obvious question. "What do you mean?"

"Trevor's here," she said. "Always figured you'd be back someday."

Robin understood. "It was you," she said. "The person taking care of his grave. When I went, there were flowers that weren't two days old."

"No one thinks about the cemetery this long after," Cindy said. "Didn't sit right, letting it go. Even I'm allowed to say a prayer now and then."

At the front of the gallery, Micheline raised her glass, and the crowd raised theirs in response, a sea of garnet and ivory winking in the glitter and golden lights. The room was warm. Women began piling their handbags in a corner, settling in for more wine and talk. Robin spotted Micheline, flushed, at the center of a crowd, gesturing toward a set of ink drawings on the wall.

Things could be different. And they were. Piece by piece, Four Points would turn for the better, emerging from its squalor as something brighter, promising. Its story—Robin's story—wasn't over. Robin had left somewhere in the middle, at the darkest point, the sad strands dangling even as she built another faraway life. She gathered them now, tied them neatly. She didn't know what would happen, but she could move on from here whole.

A space in front of her cleared as a group moved to the front for more wine, revealing Vincent: wearing his black wool coat, studying a photograph of the Jumon-ville Cross high on Chestnut Ridge. He turned, meeting her eye across the room, and lifted his chin. For a long moment, she held his gaze. He knew everything about her. He'd seen her at her worst, had humiliated and hurt her, had driven her to the greatest mistakes of her life. Yet the world didn't end when he saw her. It wouldn't end when they crossed paths again. He raised his glass, slightly, and she raised hers. Then each of them turned away.

*   *   *

It was past eleven when Robin returned to the house. Cindy, Amber, and Haley had left earlier, but Robin had stayed to help Micheline close up. The lights in the house on Whistlestop Road were on, and Robin knew Haley and Dana would be watching a movie inside, waiting for her. She pulled smoothly to the curb. At the sound of her slamming door, the Dobermans raced to the fence, leaping and barking. Robin adjusted her purse on her shoulder and started along the walkway to the house. Vincent had installed a light by the door, and Dana had remembered to turn it on at sunset.

The light suddenly flickered, dimmed, died, shrouding everything in darkness and restarting the Dobermans' barking. Then it glowed on again, and with the light came a low hum. Robin unlocked the door and reached in to switch the light off. She dropped her purse at her feet and rummaged through it for the mini screwdriver set she now carried with her. She rose onto her tiptoes, loosened a few screws, and removed the lantern face and warm bulb. She felt for the loose wire she knew was within the fixture and tightened the connection, her hands working deftly without her having to see. Robin reattached the bulb and lantern, then turned the fixture back on. The light was bright and steady, illuminating the arc of Whistletop Road even after she went inside.

ACKNOWLEDGMENTS

Thanks first to Abram Himelstein, GK Darby, and Katie Pfalzgraff at UNO Press for saying yes to this story and editing it so beautifully. What an honor to work with you on a second book.

It's a gift to have early readers, and this novel has had the good fortune of excellent company along the way. Particular thanks to Shanna McNair and Scott Wolven from The Writer's Hotel and my brilliant workshop from 2017: Grace Carpenter, Julie Carpenter, Scott Branks del Llano, Michelle Harris, Jessica Lipnack, Lyndsie Manusos, Kelly Morton, Diane Oatley, and Naomi Ulsted. Your fingerprints are on the pages of this book.

My parents, Larry and Marge Orlando, have been drawn into landlording intrigue since my research for this novel led me to purchase and restore a decrepit historic house in my Pennsylvania hometown. Thanks, Mom and Dad, for always being game for just about anything. Someday, managing an eviction with me on FaceTime will be a fond family memory.

My charming children, Lucia and Greta, did not help with this book in any way, but I love them a lot.

My husband, Andrew, is my first and best supporter, reader, and voice of reason. Thank you for loving creaky, old homes, welcoming small-town adventures, and—of course—for taking such good care of us all. This book is for you.